Quest For Courage

Chronicles Of Hope, Volume 1

Cris Hoxie

Published by C&L Publishing, 2024.

QUEST FOR COURAGE

First edition. November 14, 2024.

Copyright © 2024 Cris Hoxie.

ISBN: 979-8227211392

Written by Cris Hoxie.

Dedicated to all who battle fears—may you find the courage within to face each challenge, and the faith to know that you are never alone on your journey.

For God did not give us a spirit of fear. He gave us a spirit of power and of love and of a good mind. 2 Timothy 1:7 (New Life Version)

Prologue

Becca sat alone in her room, her fingers tracing the worn edges of her favorite childhood book. The familiar stories once brought her comfort, but now they served as a reminder of the world outside—a world she found increasingly difficult to face. At seventeen, Becca's life was defined by fear. It clung to her like a shadow, whispering doubts and magnifying every worry.

Her parents, Tom and Carol, tried to help, but it wasn't easy. Tom was a man of few words, preferring to show his support through small acts of kindness. He would often sit with Becca during her worst moments, offering silent companionship when words failed. Carol, on the other hand, was a whirlwind of optimism and energy, always attempting to lift Becca's spirits with jokes and plans for family outings. Despite their efforts, a gap remained between their intentions and Becca's reality.

Becca's younger brother, Jason, was a typical fifteen-year-old, more concerned with his own world than his sister's struggles. Yet, in his own way, he cared deeply, often lingering outside her door when she was having a particularly tough day, just to make sure she was okay.

School was another battleground. The halls buzzed with the chatter of classmates, but to Becca, it was a constant reminder of her own isolation. She avoided crowded places, skipped social events, and kept her head down, hoping to blend into the background. The idea of drawing attention to herself was terrifying; the thought of failing even more so.

Yet, every Sunday morning, a small light shone through the darkness. The family attended a vibrant church, filled with teens who sang praise songs in jeans and T-shirts. It was a place where Becca could momentarily escape her fears. The new pastor had a way of speaking that made her feel seen, as if he understood the battles she fought daily. His sermons spoke of hope and courage, planting seeds of change in her heart.

Despite the church's welcoming atmosphere, Becca remained on the fringes, watching the youth group with a mix of longing and apprehension. It was easier to stay invisible than to risk rejection or failure.

But change was coming. Unknown to Becca, this church and its vibrant community would become the setting for a journey she never expected to take—a journey from fear to faith.

Chapter 1

Becca's alarm buzzed insistently, yanking her from the shallow depths of sleep. She reached out a trembling hand to silence it, her heart already racing. Mornings were the worst—another day filled with the same fears and anxieties. She took a deep breath and sat up, pushing herself to face the day.

The mirror reflected a pale, anxious girl with dark circles under her eyes. Becca brushed her hair with quick, nervous strokes, trying to ignore the flutter of panic in her chest. Her clothes were carefully chosen to blend in—nothing too bright or attention-grabbing. She wanted to be invisible.

Downstairs, the scent of coffee filled the kitchen. Her father, Tom, sat at the table, reading the newspaper. He looked up and gave her a small smile, his eyes filled with concern. Carol bustled around, packing lunches and humming a cheerful tune.

"Morning, sweetie," Carol said, placing a plate of toast in front of Becca. "Big day ahead?"

Becca shook her head, unable to meet her mother's eyes. "Just another day," she mumbled.

Tom reached out and squeezed her hand gently. "It's okay, Becca. Just take it one step at a time."

She nodded, forcing a smile, but her stomach churned with unease. The short walk to school felt like an eternity, every step weighed down by the dread of what lay ahead. She clutched her backpack straps tightly, her eyes darting around for any potential threat.

School was a racket of noise and movement, a maze of social interactions that Becca struggled to navigate. In the crowded hallways, she kept her head down, avoiding eye contact, hoping to go unnoticed. Each classroom was a minefield, every lesson a test not just of knowledge but of her ability to hold herself together.

In English class, her teacher, Mr. Davis, called on her to read a passage from the textbook. Becca's throat tightened as she stood, the pages blurring before her eyes. She stumbled through the words, her voice barely above a whisper. She could feel the eyes of her classmates on her, hear the faint whispers and snickers. By the time she finished, her face was flushed, and she sank back into her seat, wishing she could disappear.

Lunchtime offered little respite. Becca sat at the edge of a table, picking at her food, her ears tuned to the conversations around her. She envied the ease with which her peers chatted and laughed, their lives seemingly free of the paralyzing fears that ruled hers.

Math class was next, and Becca's anxiety grew with each passing minute. The numbers danced on the board, refusing to make sense. Her mind, already cluttered with fears, struggled to keep up. When Mr. Thompson called on her to solve a problem, her palms grew clammy, and her vision blurred. She stumbled through an incorrect answer, her cheeks burning with humiliation as the class erupted in laughter.

By the time the final bell rang, Becca's nerves were frayed. She practically ran home, eager to escape the day's torments. She retreated to her room, seeking comfort in the familiar confines of her sanctuary. The afternoon sun cast warm rays through the window, but even this comfort couldn't fully banish her anxiety.

That evening, as the family sat down for dinner, Carol and Tom talked about their day while Becca listened quietly, her mind preoccupied with the usual worries. After dinner, Becca retreated to her room, seeking the comfort of familiarity. She pulled out her homework, hoping to distract herself, but her mind kept wandering, unable to shake the ever-present sense of dread.

As the evening wore on, Becca tried to lose herself in a book, but the words failed to hold her attention. She put the book down and reached for her journal instead. Writing had always been her outlet, a way to process the swirling thoughts and emotions that she couldn't voice. She poured her fears onto the pages, hoping to find some clarity or relief.

By the time she closed her journal, the sky outside had darkened, and the house was quiet. She slipped under the covers, but sleep didn't come easily. Her mind churned with worry about the upcoming week, her fears magnified in the stillness of the night. What if she made a fool of herself? What if no one talked to her? What if she had a panic attack in front of everyone?

The questions swirled in her mind, unanswered, as she drifted into a restless sleep, the shadows of fear still clinging to her.

Sunday morning came with its own set of anxieties. Church was supposed to be a place of encouragement, but for Becca, it was just another social minefield. She dressed in her usual understated style, hoping to blend in and avoid drawing attention. The car ride to church was quiet, the family lost in their thoughts.

The church was bustling with activity when they arrived. Teens were milling around, chatting and laughing, their energy filling the air. Becca hesitated at the entrance, her feet feeling like lead. Carol gave her a gentle nudge.

"Go ahead, Becca. Just take it one step at a time," she said, echoing Tom's morning words.

With a deep breath, Becca stepped inside, her heart pounding. The new pastor, a friendly man with a warm smile, greeted them at the door.

"Welcome, Becca! We're so glad you could join us today," he said, his eyes full of genuine kindness.

Becca managed a small smile in return, but her anxiety spiked as she looked around at the sea of unfamiliar faces. The pastor seemed to notice her discomfort and leaned in slightly.

"Why don't I introduce yourself to the youth group?" he suggested. "They're a great bunch, and I think you'll find them very welcoming."

Becca nodded, too anxious to speak. The pastor led her over to a group of teens who were gathered around a table, chatting and laughing. As they approached, a bubbly girl with curly blonde hair and an infectious smile looked up and waved.

"Hey, Pastor John! Who's this?" she asked.

"Everyone, this is Becca. She's new to the group," Pastor John said. "Becca, this is Sarah, and these are her friends, Emily, Josh, and Alex."

Sarah's smile widened as she reached out to shake Becca's hand. "Nice to meet you, Becca! Come join us—we're just talking about the games we have planned for tonight."

Becca hesitated, but Sarah's warmth was hard to resist. She took a seat at the edge of the group, trying to blend in while observing the others. Sarah and her friends continued their conversation, occasionally turning to include Becca and making her feel somewhat welcome.

As the service began, Becca found herself gradually relaxing. The friendly atmosphere and the pastor's reassuring presence helped to chip away at her anxiety. Sarah stayed by her side, introducing her to other teens and making sure she was included in the activities.

Near the end of the service, Pastor John gathered everyone for a short talk. He spoke about the importance of community and supporting one another, his words resonating deeply with Becca. She realized she wasn't alone in her struggles—everyone had their own fears and challenges.

As the event drew to a close, Sarah turned to Becca with an excited expression. "Hey, there's another event next weekend—a small group meeting at my house. Would you like to come?"

Becca's heart raced at the thought of another social gathering, but Sarah's genuine enthusiasm and the warmth she felt from the group made her consider it. Before she could overthink it, she nodded.

"Sure, I'll come," she said, her voice steadier than she expected.

Sarah beamed. "Great! I'll text you the details."

As Becca left the church that day, she felt a mix of relief and apprehension. The service had been challenging, but she had taken a step forward. Her fears were still there, but they seemed a little less daunting with the support of her new friends.

On the car ride home, her parents didn't press her for details, sensing her need to process the experience on her own. They simply expressed their assurance and love, which meant the world to Becca.

In bed that night, Becca replayed the day's events in her mind. She had faced her fears, however small the step might have been, and it had felt liberating. With the support of her family, Pastor John, and her new friends, she began to believe that maybe, just maybe, she could overcome her fears.

As she drifted off to sleep, a new feeling settled in her chest—hope. The journey ahead would be long and difficult, but for the first time, Becca felt like she wasn't facing it alone.

Just as she was about to fall asleep, her phone buzzed on the nightstand. Groggily, she reached for it and saw a message from Sarah: "Hey Becca, there's something important I need to tell you about the small group. Can you talk now?"

Becca's heart skipped a beat. What could be so important? She hesitated, her mind racing with possibilities, before she finally typed back, "Sure, what's up?"

She waited, the seconds ticking by, each one amplifying her curiosity and apprehension. What did Sarah need to tell her? The screen lit up with Sarah's reply, and Becca's eyes widened as she read the message.

Chapter 2

Becca stared at her phone, her heart pounding as she read Sarah's message: "Hey Becca, there's something important I need to tell you about the small group. Can you talk now?" She hesitated, her mind racing with possibilities. What could be so important? Taking a deep breath, she replied, "Sure, what's up?"

Moments later, her phone buzzed again. "It's nothing bad," Sarah's message began, "but I wanted you to know that the new pastor, Pastor John, will be there. He's great and really supportive. I think you'll like him."

Relief earlier, but she hadn't interacted with him much. His friendly demeanor had been a stark contrast to the stern pastors she had known before. "Okay, thanks for letting me know," she replied, trying to sound nonchalant.

Sunday morning arrived, bringing with it the familiar blend of anxiety and anticipation. Becca dressed in her usual understated style, hoping to blend in and avoid drawing attention. Jason, her younger brother, was unusually quiet as he sat in the backseat of the car, his headphones on and his gaze fixed out the window. Carol and Tom chatted softly in the front, exchanging smiles and nods, but Becca remained lost in her own turbulent emotions.

As they arrived at church, the familiar buzz of activity was almost overwhelming. Teens and families filled the seats, chatting and laughing. Becca hesitated at the entrance, her heart pounding in her chest. Carol gave her a gentle nudge, offering an encouraging smile.

Becca took a deep breath and stepped inside. The sanctuary was bustling with energy as people settled into their seats. Jason, trailing behind Becca and their parents, looked around with mild interest before finding a spot next to their parents.

Pastor John stepped up to the podium, his presence immediately commanding attention. His warm smile and confident demeanor seemed to radiate a sense of calm. "Good morning, everyone," he greeted, his voice rich and inviting. "Today, I want to talk about fear and how it can hold us back from experiencing the fullness of life that God has planned for us."

Becca's heart skipped a beat. Fear. The very thing that had shadowed her life for as long as she could remember. She leaned forward slightly, her curiosity piqued despite herself.

Pastor John began to share his message, weaving personal stories with biblical references. He spoke of his own struggles with fear, how it had often paralyzed him, and how faith had been a guiding light through his darkest moments. His words were filled with empathy and understanding, a far cry from the judgmental tones Becca had heard in the past.

As he spoke, Becca found herself absorbed by his message. Pastor John's insights resonated with her, and she felt a flicker of hope. He spoke of fear as both a challenge and an opportunity for growth, encouraging his listeners to face their fears head-on with faith and support from their community.

Jason, sitting beside her, seemed to be paying more attention than usual. Every so often, he glanced at Becca with a look of concern, perhaps sensing her inner turmoil. For a moment, Becca felt a pang of guilt—her struggles were affecting her family, too.

When the service ended, Becca felt a mix of emotions—hope and apprehension in equal measure. The sermon had struck a chord, but she was still overwhelmed by the enormity of her fears. The idea of confronting them seemed both daunting and distant.

As the congregation began to disperse, Pastor John approached Becca and her family. "Hello, Tom, Carol," he greeted warmly. "And this must be Becca and Jason. It's great to see you again."

Becca managed a small smile, her heart racing. "Hi," she said softly.

Pastor John extended his hand to Jason. "And you must be Jason. It's nice to meet you."

Jason nodded, returning the handshake with a shy smile.

"I hope you enjoyed the service," Pastor John said, his gaze kind and attentive. "I understand it can be overwhelming sometimes, especially with new faces and experiences."

Becca nodded, appreciating his understanding but unsure of how to respond. Her parents exchanged a glance, sensing her discomfort but choosing to give her space.

Pastor John continued, "I know it can be challenging to step out of our comfort zones, but I'd love to get to know you better, Becca. If you're open to it, perhaps we could meet sometime this week for a chat?"

Becca's heart pounded even harder at the suggestion. The thought of a one-on-one meeting with the pastor filled her with both apprehension and a flicker of hope. She glanced at her parents, who smiled encouragingly.

"Sure, I think that would be okay," Becca replied, her voice barely above a whisper.

"Great," Pastor John said, his smile widening. "I'll check my schedule and give you a call to set up a time. I look forward to it, Becca."

As they left the church that day, Becca's mind was a whirlwind of thoughts and emotions. The pastor's offer to meet and talk was both terrifying and intriguing. She couldn't help but wonder what he would say and if he could truly help her navigate the fears that had long controlled her life.

Jason fell into step beside her as they walked to the car. "How was it?" he asked quietly, his voice tinged with genuine curiosity.

Becca shrugged, trying to mask her anxiety. "It was... interesting Pastor John is different. He talks about fear in a way I haven't heard before."

Jason nodded thoughtfully, his gaze drifting ahead. "That's good, right?"

Becca managed a weak smile. "Yeah, I guess so."

That night, as Becca lay in bed, her phone buzzed again. It was a message from Pastor John: "Hi Becca, it was wonderful to meet you again today. How about we meet on Wednesday after school at the church office? Let me know if that works for you."

Becca stared at the message, her heart racing with a mixture of fear and anticipation. This could be a turning point, a chance to finally confront her fears with the help of someone who seemed to genuinely care. She took a deep breath and replied, "Wednesday works for me. Thank you."

Just as she was about to put her phone down, another message popped up. It was from Sarah: "Hey Becca, I just heard something—Pastor John has been working with a few other people who have some really intense fears. I think you might find their stories really inspiring."

Becca's curiosity was piqued, but her anxiety was mounting. What did Sarah mean by "intense fears"? Was there something about Pastor John's work that she didn't know? Her mind raced with questions as she wondered how the pastor's work could affect her own journey.

The room felt colder, and the shadows on the walls seemed to grow longer. Becca stared at her phone, her fingers hovering over the screen, unsure whether to reply or to let it go for now. The uncertainties ahead seemed to loom larger, the fear of the unknown gnawing at her resolve.

With a sigh, Becca turned off her phone and placed it on the nightstand. As she lay back, her thoughts churned with anticipation and dread. What was Pastor John's work truly about, and what could it mean for her own struggles?

The questions lingered in her mind, unanswered, as she drifted into a restless sleep. Little did she know, the upcoming meeting would unearth more than she had ever anticipated, setting the stage for a journey that would challenge her fears and reshape her life.

As Becca closed her eyes, she couldn't shake the feeling that something significant was about to happen—something that would force her to confront not only her own fears but also the very core of her being. The uncertainty of what lay ahead gnawed at her, leaving her with a haunting question: What if facing her fears led to something she wasn't ready for?

A chill ran down her spine as the shadows seemed to dance on the walls, hinting at the unknown challenges that awaited her.

Chapter 3

Wednesday afternoon arrived with a mix of apprehension and reluctant anticipation. Becca found herself pacing back and forth in her room, her mind replaying snippets of Pastor John's sermon and Sarah's cryptic message. The thought of meeting Pastor John alone was both unsettling and strangely reassuring. This was her chance to confront her fears, but she was still unsure of what to expect.

At three o'clock, Becca reluctantly gathered her things and headed for the church. The streets were unusually quiet, adding to the eerie calm that seemed to envelop her. She glanced at her phone one last time to confirm the address before entering the church's office building, which was separate from the main sanctuary.

As she walked down the hallway, her footsteps echoed softly against the walls. She reached the office door and took a deep breath, trying to steady her nerves. She knocked lightly, and a warm voice called from inside.

"Come in!"

Becca turned the handle and stepped into the office. Pastor John was seated behind a desk, his calm demeanor immediately putting her at ease. He looked up from his papers with a welcoming smile.

"Hello, Becca. It's great to see you again," Pastor John said, rising to greet her. He motioned to a comfortable chair across from his desk. "Please, have a seat."

Becca sat down, feeling a mixture of nervousness and relief. Pastor John's office was cozy, with warm colors and comfortable furniture.

The soft lighting and the gentle hum of an air conditioner provided a calming atmosphere.

"Thank you for meeting with me," Becca said, her voice a little unsteady.

"Of course," Pastor John replied, his tone reassuring. "I appreciate you taking the time to come in. I know that facing our fears can be incredibly challenging."

Becca nodded, struggling to find the right words. "I've been dealing with a lot of fears for as long as I can remember. It's like there's this constant weight that keeps me from doing things I want to do."

Pastor John listened intently, his expression one of genuine empathy. "Tell me more about these fears, Becca. What are some of the things that hold you back?"

Becca hesitated for a moment, her mind racing through her anxieties. "Well, it's not just one thing. I get anxious about social situations, like meeting new people or going to places where I'm not familiar. Sometimes it feels like everything is a big, scary unknown."

Pastor John nodded, his gaze compassionate. "I understand. Fear of the unknown can be paralyzing. It's a common struggle, and it's something many people face. What's important to remember is that you're not alone in this. Facing fears is a process, and it often helps to have support along the way."

Becca looked down, her fingers fidgeting with the edge of her sleeve. "I've never really talked about this with anyone before. It's hard to open up."

Pastor John leaned forward slightly, his voice gentle. "It can be difficult to share our struggles, but doing so can be a powerful step toward healing. I want you to know that this is a safe space. Whatever you share here stays between us, and my goal is to help you work through these challenges in a way that feels right for you."

Becca felt a flicker of hope at his words. "Thank you. It means a lot to hear that."

Pastor John smiled warmly. "I'd like you to join in with a few people who might be able to offer additional support and encouragement. They're part of our youth group here at the church, and they've faced their own challenges. They meet regularly, and I think you might find their stories and experiences helpful."

Becca's heart skipped a beat. The idea of meeting with a group of people who understood what she was going through was both intriguing and terrifying. "I don't know... What if I don't fit in?"

"Everyone feels that way at first," Pastor John said reassuringly. "But you might be surprised at how welcoming and understanding they can be. Sometimes, taking that first step can lead to unexpected and positive changes."

Becca was silent for a moment, considering his words. The thought of joining the youth group was daunting, but Pastor John's encouragement made it seem like a viable possibility.

Pastor John leaned back in his chair, his expression thoughtful. "How about this: why don't you come by the youth group meeting this Friday? It's a casual gathering where we talk about our struggles and support each other. If you decide it's not for you, that's perfectly okay. But it could be a great opportunity for you to meet people who are on similar journeys. It is a little more relaxed than what you experienced before."

Becca's heart raced at the thought. She wanted to say yes, but the fear of the unknown still lingered. "I'll think about it," she said, trying to sound confident but feeling uncertain inside.

Pastor John's eyes twinkled with a hint of mischief. "You know, I think it might be helpful if you brought someone along for support. How about inviting your brother, Jason? Sometimes having a familiar face can make a big difference."

Becca's eyes widened in surprise. "Jason? He's younger, and I'm not sure he'd be interested..."

"Jason could benefit from the supportive environment as well," Pastor John said kindly. "And it might help both of you if you share the experience. It's entirely up to you, but I think it could be a good idea."

Becca thought about it for a moment. The prospect of having Jason there was both reassuring and complicated. She wasn't sure how he would react to the idea, but Pastor John's suggestion seemed to offer a potential way to ease her own anxiety.

"Okay," Becca said finally, nodding slowly. "I'll talk to Jason and see if he wants to come along."

"Fantastic," Pastor John said, his smile widening. "I'll look forward to seeing both of you on Friday. And remember, it's all about taking small steps and finding the right support."

As Becca stood up to leave, she felt a mixture of relief and apprehension. The meeting with Pastor John had been unexpectedly comforting, yet the idea of attending the youth group meeting with Jason in tow was still frightening.

She walked out of the church office, her mind swirling with thoughts. The prospect of joining the youth group with Jason was both exciting and intimidating. What if it turned out to be a chance for real change, or what if it only added to her fears?

Jason fell into step beside her as they walked to the car. "How was it?" he asked quietly, his voice tinged with genuine curiosity.

Becca took a deep breath, trying to mask her anxiety. "It was good. Pastor John wants us to come to a youth group meeting on Friday. He thinks it could help us both."

Jason raised an eyebrow. "Youth group? What's that like?"

Becca shrugged, feeling a mixture of hope and uncertainty. "I'm not sure yet, but I think it might be a good opportunity for us. Are you up for it?"

Jason considered her question, his expression thoughtful. "Yeah, I guess. If it helps you, I'll go."

Becca managed a grateful smile. "Thanks, Jason. I appreciate it."

As they drove home, Becca's thoughts were consumed with the upcoming youth group meeting. The anticipation was almost unbearable, and she couldn't shake the feeling that something significant was on the horizon.

Later that evening, as Becca was getting ready for bed, her phone buzzed with a new message. It was from Sarah: "Hey, just wanted to remind you about the youth group meeting on Friday. We're really looking forward to meeting you!"

Becca's thumb hovered over the screen as she read the message, but before she could reply, another notification popped up. It was an email from Pastor John with the subject line: "Important Information for Friday."

Becca opened the email, her heart racing. The message inside was brief but alarming: "Becca, just a heads-up—Friday's meeting might be a bit different from usual. We're having a special discussion that could be quite revealing. I believe it will be valuable for you, but I wanted to make sure you're prepared. See you then."

A shiver ran down Becca's spine. The idea of a "special discussion" made her anxious, and she wondered what kind of revelations might await her. As she stared at the email, a growing sense of unease settled over her.

Would Friday's meeting offer the support she so desperately needed, or would it uncover something even more challenging? The uncertainty gnawed at her as she prepared for bed, leaving her with a haunting question: What was Pastor John preparing her for, and how would it affect her journey toward overcoming her fears?

With a final glance at the email, Becca turned off her phone and lay back in bed. The shadows on the walls seemed to grow longer, and the anticipation of what was to come made sleep elusive.

Chapter 4

Friday arrived with an unsettling blend of anticipation and dread. Becca's thoughts were consumed by the upcoming youth group meeting. She had spent the past two days fluctuating between hope and anxiety, the special discussion mentioned in Pastor John's email looming like a dark cloud over her thoughts. She glanced at the clock and realized it was time to leave. With a deep breath, she turned to Jason, who was already waiting by the door, his expression a mix of curiosity and concern.

"You ready?" Becca asked, trying to sound more confident than she felt.

Jason nodded, though his eyes betrayed his own nervousness. "Yeah, let's go."

They drove to the church in near silence, the weight of anticipation heavy in the air. The church grounds were bustling with activity as families and young people milled about. The sight of the lively atmosphere was both comforting and intimidating. As they approached the youth center, Becca felt a flutter of nerves. She hoped that the presence of her brother might make the experience less daunting.

Upon entering the youth center, Becca scanned the room, her gaze searching for Sarah. The room was alive with energy—teens chatting, laughing, and moving between various activity stations. The vibrant decorations and casual setup created a welcoming atmosphere, but the unfamiliarity of it all made Becca's anxiety flare up.

Jason noticed her searching and put a reassuring hand on her shoulder. "You okay?"

Becca nodded, though her nerves were still on edge. "Yeah, just looking for Sarah. She said she'd be here."

Just as Becca was about to ask Pastor John for help, Sarah appeared from the crowd with a bright smile. "Hey, Becca! Over here!"

Becca's face brightened as she moved towards Sarah, feeling a wave of relief wash over her. Sarah greeted her with a warm hug, which was unexpectedly comforting.

"Hey, Sarah," Becca said, her voice tinged with a mix of nervousness and gratitude.

"I'm so glad you came!" Sarah said enthusiastically. "Let me introduce you to some of the others."

Sarah led Becca and Jason to a group of teens who were gathered around a table for an icebreaker activity. Becca felt her anxiety ease slightly as Sarah continued to include her in conversations and activities. The group was friendly, and their energy was contagious.

Pastor John gathered everyone together for the start of the meeting. His approachable demeanor immediately set a positive tone. "Welcome, everyone! Tonight, we have some fun activities planned and a special discussion on overcoming personal fears. Let's get started!"

The evening began with a series of icebreaker games designed to help everyone get to know each other. Becca participated with a hesitant but genuine effort, her nerves gradually calming as she engaged with the group. The activities were designed to be inclusive, and Becca found herself starting to relax.

During one of the games, Sarah stayed close to Becca, providing a supportive presence that helped ease her anxiety. The friendly banter and laughter of the group began to draw Becca in, and she felt a growing sense of belonging.

As the evening progressed, Pastor John led a discussion about facing personal fears and finding support within the community. The conversation was candid and open, with group members sharing their own experiences and offering encouragement to each other. Becca listened intently, finding comfort in the shared stories and the supportive atmosphere.

At the end of the meeting, Sarah approached Becca with an enthusiastic smile. "I'm really glad you came tonight. We're planning a weekend outing to the park tomorrow, and I'd love for you to join us. It'll be a great way to hang out and get to know everyone better."

Becca's heart skipped a beat at the invitation. The idea of spending more time with Sarah and the group was both exciting and nerve-wracking. She glanced at Jason, who was chatting with one of the other teens, and then back at Sarah.

"I'd love to," Becca said, trying to mask her apprehension with a smile. "I just need to check with my parents and see if it's okay."

"Great!" Sarah said with enthusiasm. "We'll be meeting at the park around ten in the morning. I'll text you the details."

As Sarah walked away, Becca felt a mix of excitement and uncertainty. The invitation was a step toward opening up and connecting with others, yet the thought of spending a whole day with new people was daunting.

Jason joined her as they prepared to leave. "So, how was it? Did you have fun?"

Becca nodded, her mind still racing with the implications of Sarah's invitation. "Yeah, it was good. Sarah invited us to a park outing tomorrow. I think I'm going to go."

Jason raised an eyebrow. "Are you sure? It sounds like it could be a lot of people."

Becca shrugged, trying to appear more confident than she felt. "Yeah, I think it might be good for me. Besides, having you there might help."

As they drove home, Becca's thoughts were a whirlwind of excitement and trepidation. The prospect of spending the day at the park with Sarah and the group was both thrilling and terrifying. What if the outing turned out to be a positive experience, or what if it only intensified her fears?

Later that evening, as Becca was getting ready for bed, her phone buzzed with a new message. It was from Sarah: "Just a reminder about the park tomorrow! We'll be doing some fun activities and hanging out. Can't wait to see you there!"

Becca's thumb hovered over the screen as she read the message, but before she could reply, another notification popped up. It was an email from Pastor John with the subject line: "Important Information for Tomorrow."

Becca opened the email, her heart racing. The message inside was brief but alarming: "Becca, just a heads-up—tomorrow's outing will include some personal sharing activities. I believe it will be valuable for you, but I wanted to make sure you're prepared. See you then."

A shiver ran down Becca's spine. The idea of personal sharing activities made her anxious, and she wondered what kind of revelations might await her. As she stared at the email, a growing sense of unease settled over her.

Would the park outing offer the support she so desperately needed, or would it uncover something even more challenging? The uncertainty gnawed at her as she prepared for bed, leaving her with a haunting question: What was Pastor John preparing her for, and how would it affect her journey toward overcoming her fears?

With a final glance at the email, Becca turned off her phone and lay back in bed. The shadows on the walls seemed to grow longer, and the anticipation of the following day made sleep elusive. The path ahead was shrouded in uncertainty, and Becca couldn't help but wonder if she was truly ready for the challenges that awaited her.

Chapter 5

Saturday morning arrived with a haze of anticipation and nerves for Becca. The sun was shining brightly, casting a warm glow over the park, but Becca felt cold sweat on her palms as she and Jason approached the designated meeting spot. The park was alive with activity—groups of people picnicking, children playing, and the occasional jogger making their way along the trails.

Becca glanced over at Jason, who was carrying a backpack filled with snacks and water. His expression was a mix of curiosity and enthusiasm. "You sure you're ready for this?" he asked, sensing her apprehension.

Becca took a deep breath, trying to steady her nerves. "Yeah, I guess. I just keep thinking about what might happen. What if it's too much?"

Jason gave her a reassuring smile. "We can always leave if it gets overwhelming. But it might be worth sticking around to see how it goes."

As they arrived at the park's picnic area, Becca spotted Sarah chatting with a group of friends. Sarah waved enthusiastically when she saw Becca and Jason approaching. "Hey! You made it! We're just getting set up over here."

Becca offered a hesitant smile and followed Sarah to the group, where a few blankets and chairs were scattered around under the shade of a large oak tree. The group welcomed them warmly, and Becca noticed how the atmosphere was already much more relaxed and inviting than she had anticipated.

The morning began with some light hearted activities. They played team games, shared funny stories, and enjoyed a picnic spread with an assortment of snacks and homemade treats. Becca slowly began to feel at ease, her nerves gradually melting away as she engaged with the group. The laughter and camaraderie helped her feel more comfortable in this new environment.

Jason, meanwhile, had gravitated toward a group of boys who were engaged in a lively game of frisbee. He was quickly pulled into their game, his earlier nerves dissipating as he began to enjoy himself. Becca watched him from a distance, feeling a small sense of relief that he seemed to be fitting in well.

As the day continued, Becca and Sarah found themselves sitting together on a blanket, sharing more personal stories and getting to know each other better. Sarah's warmth and genuine interest made it easier for Becca to open up. They talked about their favorite books, movies, and the challenges they faced in their lives. Becca found herself laughing and enjoying Sarah's company more than she had expected.

Later in the afternoon, Pastor John gathered everyone together for a more reflective part of the outing. They were still under the oak tree, the casual atmosphere of the park contrasting with the deeper tone of the conversation about to take place.

"We've had a lot of fun today," Pastor John said, his voice carrying across the picnic area. "But now I'd like to shift gears a bit. Part of our journey is about sharing and supporting one another, especially when it comes to our personal challenges and fears."

Becca's heart skipped a beat. The idea of sharing something personal in front of the group was intimidating. She had been hoping to avoid this part of the outing, but now it seemed inevitable.

Sarah noticed Becca's apprehensive expression and placed a reassuring hand on her shoulder. "It's okay," Sarah said softly. "You don't have to share anything you're not comfortable with. Just listen and share if and when you're ready."

Pastor John began by sharing his own story, detailing his experiences with fear and personal growth. His vulnerability and openness made the atmosphere feel safer, but Becca still felt a knot of anxiety in her stomach.

As others in the group began to share their own experiences, Becca felt a mixture of inspiration and dread. Each story was met with empathy and support, and Becca's initial apprehension began to waver. The sense of community was strong, and it became clear that this was a space where people were encouraged to be open and supportive.

Jason, who had rejoined Becca after the frisbee game, was quietly listening to the conversation. Becca glanced at him, noting how attentive he was. To her surprise, Jason raised his hand and spoke up.

"I'd like to share something too," Jason said, his voice steady but tinged with vulnerability. "I've been struggling with my own fears lately. I didn't really talk about it before, but..."

Becca's eyes widened. She hadn't realized Jason was dealing with his own set of challenges. She listened intently as Jason opened up about his fears of not measuring up in school and feeling overshadowed by Becca's own struggles. It was a side of him she hadn't seen before, and it made her heart ache.

Jason continued, his voice filled with honesty. "Sometimes I feel like I'm not good enough, and it's been really tough trying to keep up with everything. I didn't want to burden anyone with it, but it's been weighing on me."

The group listened with empathy, and Becca saw how Jason's admission was met with understanding and support from the others. She felt a mix of emotions—admiration in her brother's bravery and a new sense of connection with him.

As the discussion continued, Pastor John turned to Becca with a kind, encouraging smile. "Becca, would you like to share something with the group? We'd love to hear your story, but only if you feel ready."

Becca's breath caught in her throat. Her heart pounded as she looked around at the expectant faces of the group. The thought of sharing her fears and struggles was overwhelming.

Jason, who had just opened up about his own struggles, gave her a supportive look. "You don't have to if you're not ready," he said quietly.

Becca nodded, her mind racing. The invitation to share felt like both an opportunity and a daunting challenge. The park's tranquil surroundings were a stark contrast to the storm of emotions she was experiencing.

As Becca considered the choice before her, the gravity of the moment settled over her. The invitation to share was a significant step toward vulnerability and connection, but it also posed a fearsome challenge.

Would she be able to open up and take this crucial step toward overcoming her fears, or would she retreat and miss an opportunity for deeper connection? The uncertainty weighed heavily on her as she prepared to make her decision.

The group waited in respectful silence, their attention focused on Becca. The tension in the air was palpable as she stood on the verge of sharing her story or remaining silent.

Becca took a deep breath, her eyes darting between the supportive faces of the group and the comforting presence of Sarah. As she opened her mouth to speak, her voice faltered, and she could feel the weight of the moment bearing down on her.

The decision of whether Becca would share or retreat loomed large, leaving her with a critical choice that could shape her journey forward. The future of her connection with the group—and her personal growth—hung in the balance as she faced the moment of truth.

With the park's gentle breeze rustling the leaves above and the sun casting colorful shadows on the grass, Becca faced the most pivotal decision of her journey: would she embrace the opportunity to share and connect, or would she hold back and stay within her shell?

Chapter 6

The sun had begun its descent, casting a golden hue over the park as Becca sat with the group. The warmth of the afternoon had softened her anxiety, but the weight of the decision to share her fears was still heavy on her shoulders. Sarah, noticing Becca's discomfort, shifted closer, her presence a calming force.

"You don't have to do this if you're not ready," Sarah whispered, her voice gentle and encouraging. "But just know that everyone here is really supportive.

Becca took a deep breath, her gaze shifting between the supportive faces of the group and the serene park surroundings. Her hands trembled slightly as she clasped them together in her lap. The fear of vulnerability and judgment gnawed at her, but the open and accepting atmosphere of the group offered a glimmer of hope.

Pastor John, who had been quietly observing, offered Becca a reassuring nod. "Whenever you're ready, Becca. No rush."

The rustling of leaves in the breeze seemed to underscore the significance of the moment. Becca's heart pounded in her chest as she wrestled with her internal struggle. The thought of opening up felt like stepping off the edge of a cliff, with only the hope of a soft landing to guide her.

Sarah placed a comforting hand on Becca's back. "You can do this. You don't have to share everything, just what you're comfortable with."

Becca's eyes met Sarah's, and for a moment, she saw nothing but genuine encouragement. With a deep breath, Becca decided to take a small but significant step. She cleared her throat and began to speak, her voice trembling but resolute.

"I... I've always been afraid of not being good enough. It's like this constant shadow that follows me, making me doubt myself. I've been scared to try new things because I'm afraid of failing."

As she spoke, the group listened in respectful silence. Becca's words were punctuated by the occasional hiccup of emotion, but the sincerity in her voice was clear. She continued, revealing bits of her struggle with social anxiety and the fear of judgment that had held her back for so long.

"I'm also afraid of disappointing people," Becca admitted, her voice cracking slightly. "Like, if I try something and it doesn't work out, I feel like I'm letting everyone down."

Sarah's hand squeezed Becca's shoulder gently, and she gave her an encouraging nod. "We understand. We all have our own fears, and it's okay to share them."

One by one, members of the group began to share their own experiences. The stories ranged from fears of failure to concerns about personal relationships. Each account was met with empathy and support, and Becca found herself feeling a bit lighter with every shared story.

Pastor John addressed the group with warmth. "Thank you all for being so open. Becca, you've taken a courageous step today, and I want you to know that we're here for you. This is what community is all about—lifting each other up and walking together through our struggles."

Becca managed a small smile, her heart feeling a bit lighter as she absorbed the support from the group. The act of sharing her fears, though challenging, had begun to break down the barriers she had built around herself. She realized that the journey of facing her fears was a shared one, filled with support and understanding.

As the day began to wind down, the group started to gather their things to head home. Becca and Sarah lingered, chatting and laughing about their favorite moments of the day. Jason joined them, his own energy high from the fun he had had with the other boys.

Sarah turned to Becca with a warm smile. "I'm really glad you came today. You did great. Tomorrow's going to be a big day at church, and I'm sure you'll handle it just fine."

Becca nodded, feeling a sense of accomplishment and renewed confidence. "Thanks, Sarah. I'm glad I came too. It feels good to have shared a bit of my fears."

As they drove home, Becca reflected on the day's events. The outing had been more challenging and rewarding than she had anticipated. The connections she had made and the small step she had taken toward opening up felt significant. Yet, there was still a lingering sense of unease as she thought about the next day.

Sunday morning arrived with a sense of both anticipation and apprehension. Becca and Jason got ready for church, the familiar routine of Sunday morning connected against the new experiences from the day before. Becca wore a simple blue dress and her favorite sneakers, trying to feel confident despite the nerves that still lingered.

When they arrived at the church, the vibrant atmosphere was as welcoming as ever. The cheerful noise of the youth group chatting and preparing for the service contrasted sharply with Becca's internal anxiety. She was eager to put her newfound courage to the test but couldn't shake the feeling of trepidation.

The service began with lively praise songs, the upbeat melodies filling the sanctuary with an infectious energy. Becca found herself singing along, her voice blending with the chorus of the youth group. The warmth and energy of the congregation were comforting, but her mind was preoccupied with the day's upcoming challenges.

After the service, Pastor John approached Becca and Jason. "How are you both feeling today?" he asked with a friendly smile.

Becca smiled back but felt a twinge of nervousness. "I'm doing okay. Yesterday was really eye-opening."

Pastor John's eyes twinkled with understanding. "I'm glad to hear that. Remember, tomorrow is a new opportunity. Whatever challenges come your way, you're not facing them alone."

Becca nodded, appreciating the pastor's encouragement. As they prepared to leave the church, Sarah approached Becca with a thoughtful expression.

"Hey, I wanted to check in with you. How are you feeling about your presentation tomorrow?"

Becca hesitated, her anxiety about the school presentation returning. "I'm really nervous. I know it's just a presentation, but the thought of speaking in front of everyone makes me so nervous."

Sarah offered a reassuring smile. "You've made so much progress already. I know you can do this. Just take it one step at a time, and remember that everyone here believes in you."

Becca appreciated Sarah's support, but the weight of the upcoming presentation was still heavy. As they left the church and headed home, Becca's mind was a whirlwind of thoughts about the school presentation.

Monday was just around the corner, and with it came the first period of the school day where her presentation was scheduled. Becca's heart raced as she thought about the looming challenge. She knew this was more than just an assignment; it was a test of the courage she had been trying to build. The uncertainty of how she would fare in the presentation, combined with the recent progress she had made, created a storm of anticipation and dread.

As the weekend drew to a close, the reality of Monday's presentation loomed larger than ever. Would Becca be able to channel her newfound courage into her presentation and face her fears head-on, or would the anxiety overwhelm her, overshadowing the progress she had made?

Chapter 7

The alarm clock buzzed loudly, pulling Becca from a restless sleep. She groaned, feeling the weight of the school day pressing down on her. Today was different from the rest; it was the aftermath of her first real step toward confronting her fears. As she got ready, her mind raced with thoughts of her presentation and the mixed emotions that had followed.

In the kitchen, Jason was already eating breakfast, his usual cheerful self. "Morning, Becca! Ready for another day?"

Becca managed a small smile. "I guess so, Jason. Yesterday was... a lot."

Jason nodded, his eyes filled with understanding. "You did great, though. I'm proud of you."

Their mother, Carol, handed Becca a piece of toast. "Remember, honey, you can do anything you set your mind to."

Becca appreciated the encouragement but couldn't shake the nervousness that lingered. As they walked to school, Sarah caught up with them, her presence a comforting reminder of the support she had.

The school day started uneventfully, but by lunchtime, Becca's anxiety spiked. She had forgotten to prepare for an important science test, and now she felt the pressure mounting. In the cafeteria, Sarah noticed her friend's distress.

"Hey, what's wrong?" Sarah asked, her brow furrowing in concern.

"I forgot about the science test," Becca admitted, her voice barely above a whisper. "I don't think I can do this."

Sarah placed a reassuring hand on Becca's shoulder. "It's okay. I know you can do this. Remember what Pastor John said? Take it one step at a time."

Becca nodded, trying to steady her breathing. She thought back to the advice Pastor John had given her about facing challenges. "Face them head-on, and remember you're not alone," he had said. The words echoed in her mind, offering a sliver of hope.

The bell rang, signaling the start of the next period. Becca felt a knot in her stomach as she entered the science classroom. The test was placed in front of her, and she took a deep breath, trying to focus on the questions. The fear of failure loomed large, but she pushed through, remembering the support of her friends and family.

After what felt like an eternity, the test was over. Becca handed it in, her hands trembling slightly. She felt drained but relieved. As she left the classroom, Sarah was waiting for her in the hallway.

"How did it go?" Sarah asked, her eyes filled with concern.

"I think it went okay," Becca replied, her voice wavering. "Thanks for being there for me."

Sarah smiled. "Always. We stand together."

The rest of the school day passed in a blur, but Becca felt a growing sense of accomplishment. She had faced another fear and survived. When the final bell rang, she felt a mix of exhaustion and relief.

After school, Becca met up with Sarah and Jason at their usual spot in the courtyard. Jason was chatting animatedly with a group of boys from his class, his usual energy infectious. Becca watched him for a moment, marveling at how easily he connected with others. She wished she had that same confidence.

Sarah nudged her gently. "You okay?"

Becca nodded, a small smile playing on her lips. "Yeah, I think so. It was a tough day, but I'm glad I made it through."

They walked home together, the conversation light and easy. Becca felt the tension of the day slowly melting away, replaced by a sense of friendship and support. When they reached Becca's house, Sarah gave her a hug.

"Remember, if you ever need to talk, I'm here," Sarah said, her eyes full of sincerity.

"Thanks, Sarah. I appreciate it," Becca replied, feeling a warmth in her heart.

That evening, Becca sat at her desk, reflecting on the day's events. She realized she had applied what she had been learning from Pastor John and the youth group. Each small step was building her confidence, bit by bit. The thought brought a sense of peace she hadn't felt in a long time.

Just as she was about to turn in for the night, her phone buzzed with a message. It was from Pastor John. "Hi Becca, just wanted to let you know about an upcoming event. We're planning a mission trip soon, and I think it could be a great opportunity for you. Let's talk more at church on Sunday."

Becca's heart skipped a beat. A mission trip? The idea was both thrilling and terrifying. It felt like another massive challenge, but also an opportunity for growth. She stared at the message, feeling a mix of fear and excitement.

As she lay in bed, thoughts of the mission trip swirled in her mind. Could she really take this next step? The unknowns were daunting, but the support from her friends, family, and Pastor John gave her a glimmer of hope. The decision to join the mission trip would be another pivotal moment in her journey from fear to faith.

The next morning, Becca woke up with the mission trip still on her mind. At breakfast, she decided to bring it up with her family. "Mom, Dad, Pastor John called last night and mentioned a mission trip. He thinks it could be a good opportunity for me."

Tom looked at her with a mixture of surprise and pride. "A mission trip? That sounds like an incredible experience, Becca. Do you think you're ready for it?"

"I don't know," Becca admitted. "It's a big step, and I'm scared. But I think it could help me grow."

Carol smiled warmly. "Whatever you decide, we'll support you. Just take your time to think it over."

Throughout the day, Becca couldn't shake the thought of the mission trip. At school, she found herself daydreaming about the possibilities, the people she could meet, and the experiences she could have. But the fear of the unknown lingered, casting a shadow over her excitement.

After school, Becca and Sarah met up again. "So, did you think about the mission trip?" Sarah asked.

"Yeah, I did. I'm still not sure, but I'm leaning towards going," Becca replied, her voice filled with uncertainty.

Sarah grinned. "I think it would be amazing opportunity, Becca. It's a chance to step out of our comfort zones and see the world from a different perspective."

As they walked home, Becca felt a sense of determination growing within her. She knew it wouldn't be easy, but the mission trip represented a chance to continue her journey. With the support of her friends, family, and Pastor John, she felt ready to take that next step.

On Sunday, Becca and her family arrived at church, the vibrant atmosphere a comforting backdrop to her swirling thoughts. During the service, Pastor John spoke about the upcoming mission trip, his words filled with enthusiasm and hope.

"Mission trips are a chance to serve others and grow in your faith," he said, his gaze sweeping over the congregation. "It's an opportunity to step out of your comfort zone and make a difference in the world."

After the service, Becca approached Pastor John. "I'd like to talk more about the mission trip," she said, her voice steady despite the nerves.

Pastor John smiled warmly. "Of course. Let's sit down and discuss it. I think it could be a wonderful opportunity."

As they talked, Becca felt her fears begin to melt away, replaced by a sense of purpose and excitement.

The conversation with Pastor John was encouraging, his words a beacon of hope. "This trip will be transformative, Becca. You'll learn so much about yourself and your faith. I'm confident you can do it."

Becca nodded, feeling a newfound resolve. "Thank you, Pastor John. I'm still scared, but I think I'm ready."

As she left the church, Becca felt a mixture of fear and anticipation. The mission trip was a daunting prospect, but it also represented the next chapter in her journey.

Later that night, as she lay in bed, her phone buzzed again. This time, it was a message from an unknown number: "Becca, there's something you need to know about the mission trip. Call me ASAP."

She stared at her phone, her heart pounding. What could this possibly mean?

Chapter 8

Becca's mind was a whirlwind of thoughts as she lay in bed, staring at the ceiling. The events of the past few days had been overwhelming, and now this—an unexpected call about the mission trip. She took a deep breath and picked up her phone, pressing the call button with trembling fingers.

"Hello?" she answered, trying to keep her voice steady.

"Hi, Becca, it's Pastor John," came the familiar voice. "I hope I'm not calling too late."

Relief washed over her. "No, it's fine, Pastor John. What's going on?"

"I wanted to talk to you about the mission trip," he said. "I know it's a big decision, and I thought we could go over the details and any concerns you might have."

Becca's heart raced. "Okay, thank you. I appreciate that."

The next day at school, Becca found it hard to concentrate. Her mind kept drifting to the conversation with Pastor John and the daunting prospect of the mission trip. As the final bell rang, she felt a mix of comfort and apprehension. She gathered her things and headed to the park where she and Sarah had planned to meet.

When she arrived, Sarah was already there, sitting on a bench and waving her over with a warm smile. "Hey, Becca! How was your day?"

"It was okay," Becca replied, sitting down beside her. "But I've been thinking a lot about the mission trip."

Sarah's eyes lit up with excitement. "Oh, it's going to be amazing! I've been on a couple of mission trips before, and they've been life-changing."

Becca sighed. "I know it sounds great, but I'm really scared. It's such a big step, and I don't know if I'm ready to do this yet."

Sarah placed a reassuring hand on Becca's shoulder. "I understand, Becca. I felt that way the first time, too. You have been so brave lately. This could be an incredible chance for you to grow even more."

Becca nodded, though her doubts lingered. "Pastor John wants to meet with me to talk about it. I'm just not sure what to do."

"Why don't you talk to him after school tomorrow?" Sarah suggested. "He's really good at listening and giving advice.

Becca smiled, feeling a bit more at ease. "Thanks, Sarah. I think I'll do that."

The following day, Becca met with Pastor John in his office after school. He greeted her with a warm smile and invited her to sit down.

"I know the idea of the mission trip might be overwhelming," Pastor John began. "But it's an opportunity to trust in God's plan. What are your main concerns?"

Becca took a deep breath. "I'm scared of the unknown. Traveling to a new place, meeting new people, and taking on responsibilities—it's all seems just too much."

Pastor John nodded understandingly. "It's natural to feel that way, Becca. But remember, you not alone. The entire youth group will be there to support each other. And sometimes, stepping into the unknown can lead to the most amazing experiences."

"I know," Becca said softly. "But it's hard to see past the fear."

"Let's take it one step at a time," Pastor John suggested. "Think about the reasons why you might want to go on the mission trip. What positive outcomes could come from it?"

Becca pondered this for a moment. "I guess I could grow stronger in my faith and learn to trust God more. And maybe I could help others and make a difference."

"Those are great reasons," Pastor John said with a smile. "And I believe you have the strength to do it. You've already shown so much courage."

Becca felt a glimmer of hope. "I'll think about it. Thank you, Pastor John."

Later that evening, Becca sat on her bed with the mission trip brochure spread out in front of her. The images of smiling children and community projects looked inspiring, but the fear gnawed at her insides. She thought about what Pastor John and Sarah had said, and about Jason, who had been so excited but was a year too young to go.

Jason knocked on her door and entered, his eyes bright with curiosity. "Hey, Becca. Are you really thinking about going on the mission trip?"

"I'm not sure yet," Becca admitted. "It's such a big step, and I'm scared."

Jason sat beside her. "I wish I could go with you. It sounds amazing. But even if I can't, I think you should do it. You've been so brave lately. I believe in you."

Tears welled up in Becca's eyes. "Thanks so much. That means a lot."

The next morning at school, Becca still felt a mix of fear and determination. She couldn't focus on her classes, her mind preoccupied with the mission trip. During lunch, she found Sarah and they sat together in a quiet corner of the cafeteria.

"I'm still scared, Sarah," Becca confessed. "But I talked to Pastor John, and he helped me see the positive side of it."

Sarah smiled. "I'm glad to hear that. Just remember, you don't have to make a decision right away. Take your time and pray about it."

Becca nodded, feeling a bit more at ease. "I will. Thanks, Sarah."

As they talked, Becca felt her fears slowly beginning to melt away. Sarah's encouragement and Pastor John's words echoed in her mind, helping her to see the possibilities beyond her fears.

That evening, Becca approached her parents. "I've decided to consider the mission trip," she said, her voice steady despite her nerves. "I'm still quite nervous, but I think it could be a good opportunity for me."

Carol smiled warmly. "We're proud of you, Becca. This is a big step, and we know you can do it."

Tom nodded in agreement. "You've shown so much courage lately. I'm in awe of what you've achieved."

Becca felt a mixture of fear and relief. As she lay in bed that night, her phone buzzed with a message from Sarah. "Guess what? I talked to Pastor John, and I'm going on the mission trip too! We'll be there together!"

Becca's heart leaped. Sarah's companionship was the reassurance she needed, making the daunting task seem a little less intimidating. But just as she started to relax, her phone buzzed again. This time, it was a notification from the school: "Important notice: All students are required to attend a mandatory meeting on Monday regarding new policy changes."

Becca's heart sank. A mandatory meeting? What could it be about? She felt a knot of anxiety forming in her stomach, the fear of the unknown once again rearing its head. With the mission trip looming and now an unexpected school meeting, the challenges seemed to be piling up.

Chapter 9

The Monday after the unsettling message from the school, Becca felt the weight of the world on her shoulders. The mandatory school meeting and the upcoming mission trip, both scheduled for the same day, loomed like ominous clouds over her. The stress of juggling both events felt almost overwhelming.

Monday afternoon, Becca and Sarah met at their usual spot in the park. The gentle rustle of leaves and the distant laughter of children playing provided a temporary escape from their mounting anxiety.

"Hey, Sarah," Becca said, her voice betraying her worry as she sat beside her friend. "How are you holding up with everything?"

Sarah's brow was furrowed with concern. "Honestly, I'm feeling pretty stressed. It's a lot to manage, with the school meeting and the trip both on the same day. I'm worried about how we're going to handle it."

Becca nodded, feeling a pang of sympathy. "It feels like there's just too much to juggle. The trip is supposed to be a big step for me, but now it's overshadowed by all this stress."

Sarah squeezed Becca's hand reassuringly. "We need to find a way to manage both. Maybe we should talk to Pastor John. He's been so understanding and helpful. Maybe he can give us some advice on how to handle this."

Becca's face brightened slightly at the suggestion. "That's a great idea. If anyone can help us sort this out, it's him."

Later that evening, Becca and Sarah arrived at the church for their youth group meeting. The vibrant atmosphere of the church provided a brief respite from their worries. The group was abuzz with excitement about the upcoming mission trip, but Becca and Sarah were preoccupied with their own concerns.

After the group's initial activities, Pastor John approached them, his perceptive eyes catching their subdued expressions.

"How are you both doing?" he asked with a warm, concerned tone.

Becca took a deep breath. "We're having a hard time. The school meeting is the same day as the trip, and we're struggling to figure out how to manage both."

Sarah nodded in agreement. "We were hoping you could help us. We're feeling a bit overwhelmed, and we don't know how to balance everything."

Pastor John's expression softened with empathy. "I understand how challenging this must be. How about this—let me write a letter to the school explaining your situation and requesting an alternative arrangement. It might help to have some flexibility with the meeting schedule so you can focus on the trip."

Becca and Sarah exchanged relieved glances. "That would be incredible," Becca said gratefully. "Thank you, Pastor John."

The next morning, Pastor John diligently wrote a letter to the school, outlining the importance of the mission trip and requesting a possible adjustment to the mandatory meeting schedule. The letter was clear, heartfelt, and aimed at explaining the significance of the trip to Becca and Sarah.

Later that day, Becca and Sarah took the letter to the school office. The administrators reviewed it carefully and assured them they would consider the request. The waiting game began as they left the office, their hopes pinned on the school's decision.

The day before the trip, Becca and Sarah eagerly checked their email for a response from the school. Becca's heart raced as she saw a new message in her inbox. She opened it with trembling fingers, her eyes scanning the words:

"After reviewing your request, we have decided to provide an alternative arrangement for the mandatory meeting. You will be able to attend the mission trip as planned. We appreciate your proactive communication and wish you the best on your trip."

Becca's face lit up with a mixture of relief and joy. "They approved it! We can go on the trip without having to worry about the meeting!"

Sarah's face mirrored Becca's excitement. "This is amazing! I am so glad we can go!"

With the school issue resolved, Becca began to feel a sense of calm and anticipation as she packed for the trip. The support from Pastor John and the positive response from the school had lifted a significant burden from her shoulders. She started to look forward to the adventure ahead, her earlier anxiety slowly being replaced by excitement.

As she packed her bag, Becca's phone buzzed with a new message. It was from Pastor John:

"Hi Becca, just a quick reminder that tomorrow's departure will be early. We're meeting at the church at 6 AM sharp. Also, please remember that there will be a team meeting right before we leave. It's important for final preparations."

Becca read the message, nodding to herself. She set her phone aside, feeling a cautious optimism. The challenges of managing the school meeting were resolved, but a nagging worry lingered. Despite the relief, she couldn't shake the feeling that there might be unexpected challenges still ahead.

As she finished her packing and prepared for bed, Becca felt a mixture of anticipation and unease. The mission trip was just around the corner, and despite her relief over the school's response, a sense of foreboding settled over her. She tried to push it aside, focusing instead on the excitement of the trip.

She lay in bed, her mind racing with thoughts of the upcoming adventure. The anticipation was palpable, but so was an unsettling feeling that something was amiss. As she drifted off to sleep, Becca couldn't help but feel that the journey ahead would bring more than just the excitement she was looking forward to.

The next morning, as Becca and Sarah prepared to head to the church for their early departure, the sun rose with a promise of new beginnings. However, a lingering doubt hovered in Becca's mind, casting a shadow over her excitement. Little did she know, the mission trip was only the beginning of a journey that would test her resolve in ways she hadn't anticipated.

Chapter 10

As Becca and Sarah arrived early at the church, they were greeted by the usual buzz of activity. Fellow youth group members were busy loading supplies and organizing gear for the trip. Becca's heart raced with a mix of anticipation and anxiety, her doubts still gnawing at her despite the recent relief from the school's scheduling conflict.

Pastor John approached them with a warm smile. "Good morning, everyone! Before we set off, I'd like to introduce someone new who will be joining us on this mission trip." He gestured to a girl standing beside him. "This is Emma."

Emma stepped forward, her red hair shining in the morning light. She seemed shy, her eyes darting around as she gave a small wave. "Hi, everyone," she said softly. "I'm excited to be here, though I'm a bit nervous, too."

Becca felt a chord of familiarity in Emma's mannerisms. She had been in Emma's shoes not long ago. "Hi, Emma," Becca said with a reassuring smile. "I'm Becca, and this is Sarah. I know exactly how you're feeling. We're here to support each other."

Emma's eyes softened with relief. "Thanks, Becca. It really helps to know I'm not alone."

As they loaded their bags onto the bus, Becca, Sarah, and Emma settled into a row together. The bus ride was filled with chatter and excitement as the youth group discussed their plans for the trip. Emma, though quieter than the others, began to relax, gradually joining in the conversations.

During a break on the bus ride, Emma opened up about her own struggles. "I've always had a hard time with social situations and new experiences," she confessed. "That's why I'm so nervous about this trip. But I wanted to push myself."

Becca nodded understandingly. "I used to avoid situations that scared me too. This youth group has really helped me face my fears. I'm sure you'll find the same support here."

Sarah chimed in, "We're all in this together, Emma. You're not alone. We'll support each other."

The three girls continued to bond over their shared experiences, their laughter and stories bridging the gap between them. Becca admired Emma's courage in opening up and appreciated Sarah's unwavering support. Their friendship began to solidify as they shared their hopes and fears.

Upon arrival at the village, the group was warmly welcomed by the locals. The village, with its dirt roads and modest homes, exuded a charm that contrasted with the bustling city life they had left behind. The youth group quickly got to work, setting up their base and preparing for the various community projects.

Becca, Sarah, and Emma were assigned to help refurbish a community center. As they worked, Emma's nervousness seemed to dissipate, replaced by a newfound determination. Becca and Sarah noticed Emma's growing confidence and were genuinely pleased with her progress.

As they took a break from their work one afternoon, a local woman approached them, her face etched with worry. "Excuse me," she said, her voice trembling. "I need help. My daughter is very sick. Can you come?"

The trio exchanged concerned glances. "Of course," Becca said, standing up. "We'll help however we can."

The woman led them to her home, a small, modest dwelling on the outskirts of the village. Inside, they found a young girl lying on a makeshift bed, her face pale and sweaty. She looked no older than eight, and her labored breathing filled the room with a noticeable sense of urgency.

Emma knelt beside the bed, her initial fear now replaced with a calm determination. "We need to get her some help," she said, assessing the situation. "Does she have a fever?"

The woman nodded, tears streaming down her face. "Yes, very high."

Becca turned to Sarah. "We need to find someone who can help. Maybe Pastor John knows what to do."

Sarah nodded and quickly left to find Pastor John, while Becca and Emma stayed with the girl and her mother, offering comfort and reassurance. Becca's heart raced with a mix of concern and helplessness.

Moments later, Sarah returned with Pastor John and a local nurse who had been volunteering with the mission group. The nurse quickly assessed the situation and began administering care to the young girl, explaining the necessary steps to stabilize her.

As the nurse worked, Becca, Sarah, and Emma stayed by the family's side, offering words of encouragement and support. The atmosphere in the room was tense but hopeful. The girl's condition gradually improved under the nurse's care.

Pastor John looked at the three girls with admiration. "You've done an incredible job today. This is what our mission is all about—reaching out and helping those in need."

Becca felt a wave of accomplishment and humility. She realized that this unexpected opportunity to help someone in need had brought her, Sarah, and Emma even closer. They had faced their fears together and made a meaningful difference in someone's life.

As they walked back to the community center, Becca reflected on how far she had come. The mission trip was proving to be more than just a chance to help others; it was a journey of self-discovery and growth.

The next morning, as the sun rose over the village, Becca, Sarah, and Emma prepared for another day of work. The bond between them had strengthened, and they faced each challenge with renewed resolve.

Little did they know, the mission trip was about to present them with an even greater challenge—one that would test their friendship and their faith in ways they could never have imagined.

As they approached the community center, a new opportunity awaited them—one that would push their limits and test their commitment to their mission.

Chapter 11

The morning sun bathed the village in a warm, golden light as Becca, Sarah, and Emma began their day of work. The community center, now a hive of activity, was where the youth group would spend the next few days making improvements and assisting the locals.

Becca felt a renewed sense of purpose. The previous day's events—helping the sick girl and witnessing the immediate impact of their efforts—had ignited a spark within her. She was determined to step up and face her fears head-on. Yet, as she glanced around the bustling center, a twinge of anxiety still lingered.

"Are you okay?" Emma's voice broke through her thoughts. She stood beside Becca, her expression one of genuine concern.

Becca managed a small smile. "Yeah, I'm fine. Just a bit nervous about today."

Sarah, who was busy organizing supplies, looked up and gave Becca a supportive nod. "Becca, remember what we talked about yesterday? We are all here for each other."

As the day progressed, the youth group was divided into teams to tackle various tasks around the center. Becca, Sarah, and Emma were assigned to paint and clean the community hall. It was a big job, but they were determined to make a difference.

Becca found herself working side by side with Emma, who seemed to effortlessly strike up conversations and share laughter despite her earlier nervousness. Becca admired Emma's tenacity and found comfort in her new friend's company.

"Thanks for being here," Becca said, handing Emma a paintbrush. "I don't think I could do this without you."

Emma's eyes sparkled with warmth. "You're doing great. I've seen you push through so much already."

The day was marked by small victories. The community hall, once drab and worn, began to take on a vibrant, welcoming look. The local children who came by to help, their faces smeared with paint and smiles, added to the atmosphere of camaraderie and accomplishment.

During their lunch break, the group gathered under a large tree, its branches providing much-needed shade. Becca, Sarah, and Emma shared a light meal and reflected on their progress. Becca felt a surge of satisfaction as she looked around at the improvements they had made.

Sarah, her eyes twinkling with enthusiasm, said, "You're really coming into your own, Becca. I can see how much you've grown since we started this trip."

Becca's cheeks flushed with modesty. "I couldn't have done it without both of you. Your support has meant everything to me."

Emma, her gaze thoughtful, added, "I think we're all discovering strengths we didn't know we had. This trip has been more than just about helping others—it's been about helping ourselves too."

As they finished their lunch, Pastor John approached them, his expression serious but encouraging. "I need to talk to you three," he said. "There's something important we need to discuss."

The trio exchanged curious glances and followed Pastor John to a quieter corner of the community center. Becca's heart began to race again, wondering what could be so pressing.

"Before we get started," Pastor John said, "I want to commend you all on your hard work and dedication. You've made a real impact here."

Becca felt grateful, considering that it was a team effort. "Thank you, Pastor John. It's been an incredible experience."

Pastor John nodded. "I'm glad to hear that. However, there's something else we need to address. We've received an urgent request for help from a neighboring village. They've been struck by a recent disaster, and they're in desperate need of aid."

Becca's stomach dropped. The idea of facing another challenge so soon was distressing. She glanced at Sarah and Emma, whose expressions mirrored her concern.

"We could really use your help," Pastor John continued. "This is a significant opportunity to make a difference, but it's also a big commitment. I know it's a lot to ask of you."

The weight of the decision hung heavy in the air. Becca's mind raced with conflicting thoughts. The prospect of helping another village was both exhilarating and terrifying. Her initial excitement about the mission trip had been overshadowed by the enormity of the challenges they were facing.

Emma, noticing Becca's hesitation, took her hand gently. "Whatever we decide, we'll do it together."

Sarah nodded in agreement. "We've come this far. Why don't we see it through."

Pastor John's eyes were filled with understanding. "Take some time to think about it. We do need to make a decision soon, but I want you to be sure about your choice."

As they walked back to the group, Becca's mind was a whirlwind of emotions. The decision to help the neighboring village was looming over her, and she knew it would test her in ways she hadn't anticipated. The confidence she had gained during the trip was now being put to the ultimate test.

In the quiet moments before dinner, Becca found herself alone with her thoughts, grappling with the enormity of the decision ahead. The stakes were high, and the pressure was intense.

She knew that whatever choice she made would not only affect her but also her friends and the people they had come to help. The opportunity to assist another village could be a chance to further their mission and personal growth, but it also came with risks and uncertainties.

As night fell and the group gathered around the campfire, Becca's resolve was tested. The flickering flames cast long shadows, reflecting her inner turmoil. She knew that the final decision about whether to continue their mission would come soon, and it was a choice that could redefine her journey and the relationships she had built. Becca felt the weight of responsibility pressing heavily on her shoulders. The outcome of their mission was yet to be determined.

Chapter 12

As the last embers of the campfire faded into the cool night, Becca sat alone on a fallen log, staring into the darkness. The night air was crisp, and the only sounds were the crackling of the dying fire and the distant rustle of leaves. The decision she had to make was heavy on her shoulders, and the shadows cast by the fire seemed to mirror her inner struggle.

The mission had already brought so many challenges, and now the choice to continue to a new area hit hard. It wasn't just about changing locations—it was about stepping into a situation filled with more unknowns and uncertainties. The weight of this potential shift was pressing down on Becca, and despite the supportive presence of her friends and Pastor John, she felt alone in her fear.

As she tried to clear her mind, Becca replayed the discussions of the day. The idea of moving to the newly affected area, hit hard by a recent natural disaster, had been met with mixed reactions. Pastor John had proposed it as an opportunity to make a meaningful difference, and although the idea was admirable, it also felt overwhelming. Becca was torn between the desire to help and the fear of being over her head.

The night dragged on, and Becca's thoughts were a storm of doubt and anxiety. She knew that the final decision was imminent and that her choice could reshape her journey. Her gaze fell on the flickering campfire, its light a stark contrast to the uncertainty she felt inside.

The next morning arrived with the first light of dawn, casting a hopeful glow over the camp. Becca's eyes were puffy from lack of sleep, but she tried to mask her fatigue with an appearance of normalcy.

The team gathered for breakfast, and the air was filled with an almost tangible anticipation. The morning was critical; it would determine their next steps and Becca's role in the unfolding mission.

Sarah and Emma noticed Becca's distant demeanor. As they sat down to eat, Sarah leaned closer, her voice low with concern. "You've been quiet all morning. What's on your mind?"

Becca hesitated, her fingers absently stirring her oatmeal. "I'm trying to decide about the new area Pastor John mentioned. I want to help, but I'm really scared about it. This feels like such a huge step, and I don't know if I'm ready."

Emma, who had been quietly observing, placed a comforting hand on Becca's arm. "We're all feeling the pressure. Facing this fear could be a big part of your journey."

Pastor John, sensing the unease among the group, approached with a reassuring smile. "I know this is a tough decision. But think of it as an opportunity to grow and to make a real difference. You've shown incredible strength already."

Becca looked at Pastor John, feeling a mixture of fear and determination. She knew that staying in her comfort zone was no longer an option. The new area might be a challenge, but it also represented a chance to make a meaningful impact. After a moment of silence, she made her decision.

"I want to go," Becca said, her voice steady despite the trembling of her hands. "I want to help in the new area. It's a chance to face my fears head-on and to do something significant."

The team erupted in support, and Pastor John's approving nod was a source of encouragement. As they began to prepare for the new assignment, Becca felt a surge of relief mixed with apprehension. She knew the road ahead would be challenging, but the support from her friends and the clarity of her decision provided a sense of purpose.

Throughout the day, the preparations for the new assignment intensified. Becca and her friends worked tirelessly, packing supplies and reviewing plans. The atmosphere was charged with a blend of excitement and nervous energy. Becca threw herself into the preparations, using the busyness as a way to channel her nervous energy.

As the final hours before departure approached, Becca found herself battling with last-minute doubts. She was excited about the potential to help but was also overwhelmed by the magnitude of the task ahead. The new area was known for its devastation, and the thought of stepping into such a dire situation filled her with concern.

Late in the afternoon, Becca sat down with Sarah and Emma, who were taking a break from packing. The three friends shared a moment of fellowship, their conversations laced with a mix of light-heartedness and seriousness.

"Are you sure you're okay with this?" Sarah asked, her eyes searching Becca's face for signs of hesitation.

"I think so," Becca replied, her voice wavering slightly. "I'm just really nervous. What if I can't handle it? What if I let everyone down?"

Emma squeezed Becca's hand, offering a supportive smile. " It's okay to be scared. We all are. But we are not alone, and you are a lot stronger than you think."

As the sun began to set, casting long shadows across the camp, Becca's anxiety grew. The final preparations were complete, and the team was ready to depart. Becca's mind was a whirlwind of emotions as she prepared for the next phase of the mission.

In the final moments before departure, Becca found herself standing at the edge of the camp, her heart pounding with a mixture of fear and excitement. The journey ahead was uncertain, and the challenges were immense. As the team gathered their belongings and prepared to leave, Becca's doubts lingered, casting a shadow over her resolve.

As she glanced at Sarah and Emma, who stood beside her with encouraging smiles, Becca knew that the true test of her resolve was just beginning. The departure was imminent, and the path ahead was filled with uncertainty. Becca's final doubts swirled in her mind, and the weight of the decision pressed heavily on her shoulders.

With a deep breath, Becca stepped forward, ready to face the new challenges and opportunities that lay ahead. The departure was a pivotal moment, and Becca's journey was about to take a new turn—one that would test her in ways she had never imagined. The finality of the moment hung in the air, and Becca's thoughts were a mixture of fear, excitement, and anticipation as the team set out on their next adventure.

Chapter 13

The morning sun cast a golden hue over the horizon as the youth group packed their final supplies into the bus. The excitement of embarking on a new phase of their mission trip buzzed throughout the air, but Becca could only feel the knot of anxiety tightening in her stomach. The bus was soon packed to capacity with bags of clothing, non-perishable food, and various other supplies. As Becca and her friends boarded the bus, the sense of anticipation was obvious.

Sarah, seated beside Becca, sensed her friend's unease. "You look like you have a lot on your mind," she said gently, nudging Becca's shoulder.

Becca took a deep breath and forced a smile. "Yeah, I guess I'm just trying to wrap my head around everything. It's a been a lot to take in."

Emma, who was sitting on the other side of Sarah, leaned in. "We're all in this together. It's natural to feel like this, and we'll stand by each other."

Becca appreciated their support. The camaraderie within the youth group had become a cornerstone of her growing confidence. As the bus began its journey, she found herself staring out the window, watching the changing landscapes. The lush greenery of the forest gradually gave way to more open terrain and then to rugged, mountainous areas. The farther they traveled, the more the anticipation and anxiety mixed within her.

The bus ride was filled with conversations, laughter, and the occasional song, but Becca's thoughts were often interrupted by moments of quiet reflection. She couldn't shake the feeling of responsibility that lay heavy on her shoulders. The task ahead was challenging, and the reality of the situation hit her harder with every mile.

After several hours on the road, the bus finally arrived at a community center that had been set up as the mission's base camp. The building was surrounded by tents and makeshift shelters, and the damage from the recent natural disaster was evident everywhere. The center had been transformed into a hub for relief efforts, with volunteers and supplies in constant motion.

Becca's heart sank as she took in the sight of the damaged community. The once-bustling area was now a landscape of debris and disarray. Becca and the team began unloading their supplies and setting up their temporary base. The work was grueling, but it was essential.

Pastor John gathered everyone for a briefing. "We've got a lot of work ahead of us. Our main focus will be providing immediate relief—food, water, and temporary shelters. We'll also be partnering with local volunteers to help with cleanup and reconstruction efforts."

The group dispersed to their assigned tasks. Becca and Sarah were put in charge of distributing food and water to the families in need, while Emma was assigned to help with sorting and organizing donations. The first few days were a whirlwind of activity, and Becca found herself struggling to keep up with the pace. Each day brought new challenges, from managing operations to interacting with local families who had lost so much.

Despite the chaos, Becca was grateful for Sarah and Emma's unwavering support. They worked side by side, lifting each other's spirits and offering encouragement during the tough moments. Becca began to notice small changes in herself; the fear that once paralyzed her was slowly being replaced by a growing sense of determination.

One evening, after a long day of work, the team gathered around a makeshift campfire to unwind. The crackling flames cast flickering shadows on the faces of the volunteers. As they shared stories and laughter, Becca found herself opening up more about her experiences. She spoke about the challenges she faced and the fears she was working to overcome.

Emma, sitting across from Becca, nodded understandingly. "I know how you feel. I've struggled with my own fears, too. It's not easy, but facing them head-on has made a difference for me."

Sarah chimed in, "We've come a long way, Becca. Look at how much you've grown already. This mission is about more than just helping others; it's about discovering what you're capable of."

Becca felt a swell of gratitude for her friends. Their support had been a beacon of light in the midst of her uncertainty. As they talked, Pastor John approached with an important announcement. "We've received a new assignment. The local school's infrastructure was severely damaged in the disaster, and we've been asked to help with the rebuilding efforts. It's going to be a significant project, and we'll need to rally our strength and skills."

Becca's heart raced at the thought of the rebuilding project. The scale of the task was immense, and the pressure to contribute meaningfully was distressing. The thought of tackling such a massive project was both exhilarating and terrifying. Becca could feel the weight of responsibility settling over her, and the fear of not being able to meet the expectations was evident.

The next morning, the team began preparations for the rebuilding project. Becca felt a mix of apprehension and resolve as they gathered tools and materials. The challenge ahead was significant, but Becca was determined to face it head-on.

As the day progressed, Becca and her friends tackled the initial steps of the rebuilding process. They began by assessing the damage and developing a plan for the restoration of the school. The task was physically demanding and emotionally draining, but Becca was buoyed by the support of her friends and the sense of purpose that the project provided.

By the end of the day, Becca was exhausted but satisfied with the progress they had made. The rebuilding project was in its early stages, but there was a tangible sense of accomplishment among the team.Becca's fears had not disappeared entirely, but she was beginning to see that facing them was leading to growth and change.

As the sun set and the team gathered for dinner, Becca felt a deep sense of satisfaction. The project ahead was a monumental task, but she was ready to tackle it. The journey had only just begun, and there were many challenges yet to come. But with the support of her friends and the determination to make a difference, Becca felt a renewed sense of purpose.

Later that evening, as Becca sat alone by the campfire, her thoughts were interrupted by a sudden knock on the door of the community center. She glanced over to see Pastor John standing there, his expression serious. "We've just received a call from a local organization. There's been an urgent request for help with a specific aspect of the school's reconstruction. It's a task that requires immediate attention and significant effort."

Becca's heart pounded as she realized that the major task was about to begin. The nature of the request was unclear, but the urgency was evident. The weight of responsibility pressed heavily on her shoulders as she prepared to face the new challenge. The journey ahead was filled with uncertainty, but Becca was ready to face it with determination and the support of her friends.

As the team prepared to tackle the new task, Becca knew that the days ahead would be critical in defining her experience on this mission. The rebuilding project was a test of her strength and resilience, and she was determined to rise to the challenge. The journey ahead was filled with uncertainty, but Becca was ready to face it head-on, with the support of her friends and the determination to make a difference.

Chapter 14

The dawn of a new day brought with it the weight of anticipation and the sting of anxiety. Becca awoke to the sound of distant hammering and the murmur of conversations outside. The community center was already bustling with activity as volunteers from different groups worked tirelessly on various aspects of the reconstruction effort. The task that lay before Becca was dire, and she could feel the knot of fear tightening in her chest.

Pastor John had briefed the team on the new assignment: repairing the school's main hall, which had sustained significant structural damage. It was a task that required precision, skill, and a lot of hard work. The enormity of the job was tangible, and Becca's initial excitement had given way to a deep-seated fear. She had been assigned to lead a small team in the reconstruction efforts, a responsibility that felt both exhilarating and intimidating.

As Becca approached the site, she saw the remnants of the school's hall—a skeleton of exposed beams and debris. The sight was both sobering and daunting. She stood at the edge of the site, her hands clenched into fists at her sides, trying to steady her racing heart.

Sarah and Emma found her standing there, lost in thought. Sarah's eyes were filled with concern as she approached. "Are you okay, Becca? You seem really tense."

Becca nodded, though her face betrayed her unease. "Yeah, just . . . a bit. This task is huge, and I'm not really sure I'm up to it."

Emma stepped closer, placing a reassuring hand on Becca's shoulder. "It is a lot to handle. But we've faced challenges before, and we've come through stronger. You can do this."

Becca looked at Emma, who had become a source of inspiration for her. Emma's own struggle with fear had been a mirror to Becca's journey, and her encouragement had a calming effect. Becca took a deep breath, trying to muster her courage. "Thanks, Emma. I just need to push through this. I can't let fear stop me now."

Pastor John approached, his presence a calming influence. "Becca, I know this task feels huge, but you've shown tremendous growth throughout this mission. You're more capable than you realize. Take it one step at a time and remember why you're here."

Becca nodded, feeling a renewed sense of determination. The support of her friends and the guidance of Pastor John were invaluable. She took a deep breath, steeling herself for the challenge ahead. The first step was to organize her team and develop a plan for the day. The work would be intense, but it was manageable with the right approach.

The team got to work, and Becca's initial apprehension slowly began to give way to focus and determination. The task was physically demanding, but Becca found reassurance in the rhythm of the work. Each swing of the hammer, each adjustment of the beams, was a small victory in itself. As the day progressed, Becca felt a growing sense of accomplishment.

The hours flew by in a whirlwind of activity. Becca's team worked diligently, and the transformation of the main hall began to take shape. The initial damage was slowly being repaired, and the space was beginning to look more like a place of learning and community. The progress was slow but steady, and Becca's confidence grew with each completed task.

As the sun began to set, the team gathered to review their progress. The hall was still a work in progress, but the improvements were significant. Becca felt a mixture of exhaustion and satisfaction as she surveyed the site. She had faced her fear and taken on a monumental task, and the results were evident.

Pastor John gathered everyone for a brief meeting. "I'm incredibly impressed of the work you've all done. Becca, in particular, has shown remarkable growth and leadership. This is just the beginning of what we can accomplish together."

Becca felt a swell of gratitude. The journey had been challenging, but the support of her friends and the guidance of Pastor John had made a world of difference. She knew that the task was far from over, but the progress they had made was a testament to their collective effort and determination.

As the team prepared to wrap up for the day, a sudden call came through from a local community leader. "We've just received an urgent request for additional help. There's a family in need of immediate assistance, and they're struggling to rebuild their home."

Becca's heart raced as she realized that the request would require a significant commitment from the team. The urgency of the situation and the possibility of another major task were distressing. The outcome of the task they had just completed was still uncertain, and the thought of taking on more was unsettling.

The new request presented an unexpected challenge, and Becca knew that the coming days would be crucial in determining the impact of their efforts. The team had made significant progress, but the journey was far from over. Becca felt a mixture of anticipation and concern as she prepared to face the next challenge.

The team gathered around to discuss the new request. The community leader explained that the family's home had been severely damaged, and they needed immediate help with repairs. The task was complicated by the fact that the family was currently living in temporary housing, and the urgency of the situation meant that the repairs had to be completed quickly.

Becca looked around at her team, her heart heavy with the weight of responsibility and the thought of what the family was going through. The decision about how to respond to the new request would have far-reaching implications, and Becca knew that the choices they made in the coming days would be critical in shaping the outcome of their mission. She took a deep breath, her mind racing as she considered the options.

The team agreed to visit the family the next morning to assess the situation and determine the best course of action. As Becca lay in her sleeping bag that night, her thoughts were a whirlwind of concern and determination. The decision to take on the new task would test her resolve in ways she had not anticipated, and she knew that the coming days would be pivotal in defining her journey.

As the stars twinkled overhead, Becca's thoughts were interrupted by a rustling noise. She turned her head and saw Sarah and Emma sitting by the campfire, their faces illuminated by the flickering flames. They seemed to be deep in conversation, and Becca could sense the weight of the decision that lay ahead.

She quietly joined them, her heart pounding as she listened to their discussion. Sarah's voice was filled with a mix of apprehension and determination. "This is going to be a huge undertaking. I'm not sure what to expect, but I know we have to do something. I know I would want someone to do something if it was my home."

Emma nodded in agreement. "That's right. We can't back down now. If we can help this family, we should. It's what we came here to do."

Becca looked at her friends, feeling a surge of gratitude for their unwavering support. They had been with her through every step of this journey, and their encouragement was a source of strength. She knew that the decision to take on the new task would be challenging, but with their support, she felt more prepared to face whatever lay ahead.

As the fire crackled and the night grew quiet, Becca's thoughts turned to the family in need. She could picture their struggles and the impact that their help could make. The task ahead was formidable, but it was also an opportunity to make a difference in a meaningful way.

The next morning, the team set out to visit the family's home. The drive was filled with a mixture of anticipation and worry, and Becca could feel the weight of the responsibility pressing heavily on her shoulders. When they arrived, the sight of the damaged home was both sobering and heartbreaking. The family's situation was dire, and the need for assistance was clear.

Becca's team began to assess the damage and develop a plan for the repairs. The work was demanding, and the challenges were numerous. Becca felt a mix of apprehension and determination as she faced the new task. The outcome of their efforts would have a profound impact on the family and the community, and Becca knew that every decision they made would be crucial.

As they began the repairs, Becca felt a growing sense of purpose and resolve. The task was difficult, but it was also an opportunity to demonstrate the growth and strength she had gained throughout the mission. The support of her friends and the guidance of Pastor John were invaluable, and Becca was determined to make the most of the opportunity.

As the day drew to a close, Becca stood back and surveyed the progress they had made. The repairs were coming together, and the home was beginning to take shape. Becca's heart swelled with gratitude as she realized the impact of their efforts.

Becca knew that the choices they make in the coming days would be pivotal in shaping the outcome of their mission. The task they had undertaken was challenging, but it was also an opportunity to make a difference in a meaningful way.

QUEST FOR COURAGE

As the sun dipped below the horizon, Becca felt a mixture of anticipation and uneasiness. The impact of their efforts was still unfolding, and the path ahead was shrouded in uncertainty.

65

Chapter 15

As the first light of dawn crept over the horizon, Becca awoke to the sound of hammers and saws in the distance. She stretched and rubbed her eyes, the memory of the previous day's hard work bringing a smile to her face. The progress they had made on the family's home was tangible, a testament to their collective effort and determination. Becca felt a sense of satisfaction as she reflected on the team's accomplishments.

Walking to the site, she was greeted by the sight of her team already hard at work. The once damaged structure was slowly transforming into a place of hope and renewal. Becca couldn't help but feel a renewed sense of self-worth and confidence. She had faced her fears head-on and had emerged stronger for it.

Emma and Sarah joined her, their faces reflecting the same sense of achievement. "Look at what we've done, Becca," Sarah said, her voice filled with awe. "This is incredible."

Becca nodded, her heart swelling with pride. "We've come a long way. We surely couldn't have done this by ourselves."

Emma smiled, her eyes shining with encouragement. "And we couldn't have done it without you. You've been amazing, Becca."

As they continued their work, Becca noticed several local community members approaching. They were curious and grateful, their faces reflecting a mix of emotions. One elderly woman, Mrs. Gonzalez, stepped forward, her eyes brimming with tears. "Thank you," she said, her voice choked with emotion. "You have no idea how much this means to us."

Becca felt a lump in her throat as she listened to Mrs. Gonzalez's words. The gratitude and appreciation from the community were overwhelming. It was a stark reminder of the impact their work was having, not just on the physical structures but on the lives of the people who called this place home.

Throughout the day, Becca and her team interacted with more community members. Each conversation reinforced the importance of their mission and the difference they were making. Becca felt a deep sense of fulfillment and purpose. She had found her place, and it was here, helping others and making a tangible impact.

As the sun began to set, casting a golden glow over the site, Becca took a moment to reflect on her journey. She had faced numerous challenges and had grown in ways she hadn't thought possible. The mission trip had been transformative, reshaping her self-image and instilling a newfound confidence.

Just as she was beginning to relax and savor the sense of accomplishment, Pastor John approached with a concerned expression. "Becca, can I talk to you for a moment?"

Becca's heart skipped a beat. The tone in Pastor John's voice was serious, and she could sense that something was amiss. "Of course, Pastor. What's wrong?"

Pastor John led her to a quieter spot, away from the hustle and bustle of the worksite. He took a deep breath before speaking. "Becca, there's been some news. Another area nearby has been affected by a landslide. They're in desperate need of assistance."

Becca's mind raced as she processed the information. The thought of another disaster so close to their current mission was overwhelming. She had just started to feel confident in her abilities, and now a new fear was rising within her. The idea of facing yet another challenging situation was unsettling.

Pastor John continued, "I know it's a lot to take in, but we need to decide on this one quickly. They need our help, and I believe you're capable of leading this effort. You've shown incredible strength and determination so far."

Becca felt a wave of anxiety wash over her. The responsibility of leading another mission was immense, and the fear of failure loomed large in her mind. She looked at Pastor John, her eyes reflecting the turmoil she felt inside.

"Do you really think I can do this?" she asked, her voice barely above a whisper.

Pastor John nodded, his gaze steady and reassuring. "I have no doubt, Becca. You've proven yourself time and time again. You have the support of your friends and the community. You are not alone."

Becca took a deep breath, trying to steady her racing thoughts. The decision to take on this new challenge was significant, but she knew that the stakes were high. The lives and well-being of people in need depended on their efforts.

As she stood there, grappling with her fears, she felt a hand on her shoulder. She turned to see Sarah and Emma standing beside her, their expressions filled with unwavering support and determination.

"Don't worry, Becca," Sarah said firmly. "Whatever you decide, we're all in this together." Emma nodded, her eyes reflecting the same resolve. "We believe in you. You've got what it takes."

Becca felt a surge of gratitude for her friends. Their support and encouragement were the anchors she needed in this moment of uncertainty. She took another deep breath, feeling a sense of clarity and determination settle within her.

"I'll do it," she said, her voice steady. "We'll help them."

Pastor John smiled, a look of appreciation and relief in his eyes. "Thank you, Becca. I know you'll lead us well."

As they prepared to embark on this new challenge, Becca felt a mixture of fear and confidence. The path ahead was uncertain, and the stakes were high. But with the support of her friends and the lessons she had learned, she was ready to face whatever came next.

The next morning, the team gathered their supplies and prepared to set out for the new mission site. The air was filled with a sense of urgency and suspense. Becca's heart raced as she thought about the challenges that lay ahead, but she knew that this was an opportunity to make a difference.

As they loaded up the vans, Becca took a moment to reflect on the experience so far. The mission trip had been a transformative experience, reshaping her self-image and instilling a newfound confidence. She had confronted her fears and emerged stronger for it.

As the vans pulled away toward the new mission site, Becca felt a sense of resolve settle within her. The challenges ahead were significant, but she was prepared to face them, step by step. The support of her friends and the lessons she had learned would guide her through whatever lay ahead.

The road ahead was uncertain, but Becca knew she had the strength and determination to navigate it. The mission was not just about rebuilding structures; it was about rebuilding lives and communities. In that, Becca had found her purpose and her place.

Chapter 16

The van ride to the new site was filled with a mix of excitement and nervous energy. Becca, Sarah, and Emma sat together, the anticipation intense. As they approached the new location, the extent of the devastation became clear. Houses were reduced to rubble, and the streets were barely recognizable beneath the layers of mud and debris.

Pastor John gathered the group once they arrived. "This is going to be one of the toughest parts of our mission. The community here needs us more than ever. Let's give it our all and remember why we're here."

The group dispersed, each member taking on different tasks. Becca, Sarah, and Emma found themselves working together to clear debris from a small street that led to the community's central area. The work was grueling, but the presence of her friends gave Becca the strength to keep going.

Throughout the day, they met several residents, each with their own story of loss and strength. One elderly woman, Maria, shared how she had lived in the area her whole life and had never seen such destruction. Her gratitude for their help was overwhelming, bringing tears to Becca's eyes.

"This place is our home," Maria said, her voice trembling. "We thought we'd lost everything, but seeing all of you here, helping us, gives us hope."

Becca squeezed Maria's hand, feeling the weight of their mission even more deeply. "We'll do everything we can to help rebuild," she promised.

As the days passed, the bond between Becca, Sarah, and Emma grew even stronger. They faced each challenge together, their friendship providing a solid foundation amidst the chaos. Emma, in particular, became a source of inspiration for Becca. Emma's quiet strength and unwavering faith were a constant reminder of the power of perseverance.

One evening, after a particularly hard day of work, the group gathered around a campfire to share their experiences. Pastor John encouraged everyone to speak from the heart, and the stories that emerged were powerful.

Sarah was the first to speak. "I was so scared when we first got here," she admitted. "But working with all of you, seeing the difference we're making, has given me so much courage. I'm pleased with what we've accomplished.."

Emma nodded in agreement. "I used to be paralyzed by fear," she said. "But being here, with all of you, has shown me that we can overcome anything when we support each other."

Becca felt a surge of gratitude for her friends and the journey they were on. She shared her own story, reflecting on how far she had come since the beginning of the mission trip. "I never thought I could do something like this," she said. "But each day, with your support, I've found strength I didn't even know I had."

As the fire crackled and the night grew darker, the sense of camaraderie and shared purpose was evident. Becca knew that they were more than just a team; they were family.

The next morning, Pastor John gathered the group for an important announcement. "Our work here is far from over," he said. "We've cleared the road, but there's still so much to be done. Today, we're going to tackle one of the biggest tasks yet: rebuilding the community center. It's a symbol of hope for the residents here, and it's vital that we get it up and running again."

Becca felt a renewed sense of determination. The community center was a beacon of hope for the residents, a place where they could gather and find support. She knew that rebuilding it would be a monumental task, but she was ready to face it head-on.

The team worked tirelessly, each member contributing their skills and strength to the project. Becca took on a leadership role, coordinating efforts and ensuring that everyone had what they needed. The work was physically exhausting, but the sense of accomplishment kept them going.

As the days turned into weeks, the community center began to take shape. Walls were erected, and the roof was secured. The residents' smiles and expressions of gratitude were the fuel that kept the team moving forward.

One evening, as they were putting the finishing touches on the center, a local leader approached them with a request. "We've heard about another area that's been hit hard by the disaster," he said. "They need help, and we were wondering if your team could assist them once you're done here."

Becca felt a pang of anxiety. The thought of moving on to another challenging task was significant, but she knew that their mission was far from over. She glanced at her friends, seeking their input.

"We need to do this," Sarah said, her voice filled with determination. "We've come this far, and we can't stop now."

Emma nodded in agreement. "This is why we're here. To help as many people as we can."

Becca took a deep breath and turned to Pastor John. "We're in," she said, her voice steady. "We'll help the other area once we've finished here."

After the conversation with Pastor John, Becca found herself lingering, unable to shake the concern gnawing at her. "Pastor John," she began hesitantly, "I'm worried about missing so much school. I've already missed so much, and I don't know if I'll be able to graduate on time."

Pastor John looked at her with understanding. "Becca, your education is important, and I understand your concern. We will make sure to communicate with your school and explain the situation. You've grown so much on this trip, and I believe that will be recognized."

His words were comforting, but the anxiety still lingered. She nodded, trying to absorb the reassurance. "Thank you, Pastor John. I just . . . I don't want to fall behind."

"You won't," he promised. "We'll figure it out."

The sense of purpose and resolve in the group was stronger than ever. They were ready to take on whatever challenges lay ahead, united in their mission to make a difference.

As they gathered for one final campfire before moving on to the next phase of their mission, Becca felt a deep sense of gratitude for the journey they had undertaken together. The challenges they had faced had forged unbreakable bonds and transformed them in ways they could never have imagined.

Just as they were beginning to relax, a sudden noise broke the silence. Becca's heart raced as she turned to see a figure approaching them, urgency in his steps. The outcome of this event would challenge the entire group in ways they hadn't anticipated.

The night was far from over, and the mission that had brought them together would continue to test their resolve and strengthen their bonds.

Chapter 17

The night was quiet except for the soft crackle of the dying campfire. The figure that approached them turned out to be a local leader, his face lined with worry. "There's a problem," he said, his voice urgent. "The river's rising fast due to the recent rains, and the nearby village is at risk of severe flooding. We need all the help we can get to reinforce the levee and evacuate those in danger."

Becca's heart sank as she looked around at her friends. Exhaustion was etched on their faces, but there was also a spark of determination. They had faced many challenges together, and this would be no different.

Pastor John quickly organized the team, splitting them into groups to tackle different tasks. Becca found herself in a group with Sarah, Emma, and a few other youth group members. Their job was to assist with sandbagging the levee to prevent the river from overflowing.

As they worked through the night, the physical toll was immense. Each bag of sand felt heavier than the last, and the cold, wet conditions made their task even more challenging. But Becca pushed through, driven by the knowledge that their efforts could save lives.

"Keep going, everyone!" she shouted, trying to keep spirits high. "We're making a difference!"

Sarah and Emma worked alongside her, their hands blistered and faces streaked with dirt, but their resolve never wavered. As they faced this challenge, each moment of struggle strengthened their friendship.The rising waters seemed relentless, but the group's determination was unyielding. Hours passed, and dawn began to break, casting a hopeful light over their efforts. They could see the results of their hard work: the levee held strong, and the floodwaters had been kept at bay.

Just as they were about to take a brief rest, another wave of urgency swept through the group. A cry for help echoed from the nearby village. Without hesitation, Becca, Sarah, and Emma rushed toward the sound. They found an elderly man trapped in his home, unable to escape the rising waters.

"Help me, please!" he called out, his voice trembling with fear.

Becca's heart pounded as she assessed the situation. The water was rising fast, and they needed to act quickly. "We have to get him out of there," she said, her voice firm.

Together, the trio waded through the waist-deep water, carefully making their way to the man. Becca took charge, coordinating their efforts to lift him out of the house and to safety. It was a grueling process, but their teamwork and determination paid off. They managed to get the man to higher ground, where he was reunited with his family.

The relief and gratitude in the man's eyes brought tears to Becca's own. "Thank you," he said, his voice choked with emotion. "You saved my life."

As they returned to the rest of the group, the sun fully rose, casting a warm glow over the exhausted but triumphant team. Pastor John gathered everyone together to acknowledge their incredible efforts.

"What you've accomplished here is nothing short of remarkable," he said, his voice full of admiration. "You've not only protected this community but also shown what true teamwork and faith can achieve."

Becca felt a sense of accomplishment and gratitude. The challenge they had faced had strengthened their bonds and deepened their faith. They had proven to themselves and each other that they could overcome anything together.

As they prepared to move on to the next part of their mission, Becca felt a newfound sense of confidence. But just as she was starting to relax, a sudden thought struck her, bringing with it a wave of anxiety.

She realized that while she had been so focused on the mission and her responsibilities, she had neglected an important aspect of her personal life. The weight of her missed schoolwork and the looming possibility of not graduating began to press down on her. The worry she had shared with Pastor John earlier now resurfaced with full force.

Later that evening, as the group gathered around for a debriefing, Becca confided in Sarah and Emma. "I'm worried that I won't be able to catch up with my schoolwork," she admitted, her voice shaky. "I've missed so much, and I'm afraid it just might be too late."

Sarah nodded in understanding. "I've been feeling the same way," she confessed. "I didn't realize how much I'd miss, and now I'm worried about falling behind too."

Emma's eyes were sympathetic as she spoke. "I'm worried about it too. I know we're doing something important here, but it's so hard to ignore the fact that we're missing so much. I feel like I'm going to have a hard time catching up, just like you."

Becca looked at her friends, feeling a mix of relief and frustration. They were all in the same boat, struggling with the same fears. "We've all worked so hard here," she said. "But what if our schoolwork suffers? What if we can't catch up in time to graduate?"

Sarah placed a reassuring hand on Becca's shoulder. "We'll figure it out. Let's talk to Pastor John and see if there's any way we can get some help with our studies. We've already proven we can handle tough situations—this is just another one."

Emma nodded in agreement. "We can support each other through this. We've made it this far, and we'll find a way to balance everything."

Despite their reassurances, Becca couldn't shake the gnawing anxiety. The reality of her academic situation loomed large, casting a shadow over her sense of accomplishment. The final decision about the next phase of their mission was approaching, and Becca knew that she had to find a way to balance her responsibilities and fears.

As the night wore on, Becca lay awake, her mind racing with thoughts of the future. The journey ahead was uncertain, and she felt the weight of the decisions she had to make pressing heavily on her. The support of her friends and the lessons she had learned from the pastor gave her strength, but the path forward was far from clear.

Just when she thought she had settled her thoughts, an unexpected issue arose: a personal crisis that demanded her immediate attention. The severity of the crisis was yet to be fully realized, but its presence was undeniable. Becca's resolve was about to be tested in ways she hadn't anticipated, setting the stage for the next crucial chapter in her journey.

Chapter 18

The morning sun cast a golden glow over the camp, but Becca felt a storm brewing within her. She couldn't shake the sense of dread that had settled in her heart after the previous night's revelations. The weight of her academic worries combined with the pressure of their ongoing mission had her on edge.

As the group gathered for breakfast, Pastor John noticed Becca's distant expression. "Becca, can we talk for a moment?" he asked gently, guiding her away from the others.

They found a quiet spot under a large tree, it's shade providing some respite from the heat. "I've noticed you seem troubled," Pastor John began. "Is everything okay?"

Becca took a deep breath, struggling to find the right words. "I'm just feeling overpowered by everything right now" she admitted. "I thought I was getting better at handling my fears, but now it feels like they're all coming back. The mission, school, everything... it's just too much."

Pastor John nodded, his eyes filled with understanding. "It's completely normal to feel like you're being weighed down, especially when dealing with so many challenges simultaneously. Remember, you have a strong support system in your friends, and we're all here for you."

Becca looked down, her fingers nervously twisting the hem of her shirt. "I know, but it feels like I'm letting everyone down. I don't want to fail at school, and I don't want to fail here either."

"Failure is a part of growth," Pastor John said softly. "It's through our struggles that we find our strength. You've already shown incredible courage by coming this far. Trust in yourself and the support of those around you."

Becca hesitated before asking, "Pastor John, have you heard anything from the school? I'm really worried about missing so much. What if I can't graduate?"

Pastor John gave her a reassuring smile. "I have just received a response from the school. They understand the importance of what you're doing here, and they're willing to work with you and the others to make sure you all stay on track. We'll go over the details together, but for now, focus on the present. You're making a difference here, Becca."

Becca took a shaky breath, the warmth of his words seeping into her heart. She felt a small flicker of hope amidst the overwhelming darkness. "I guess I just need to take it one step at a time," she said quietly.

"Exactly," Pastor John agreed. "Focus on what you can do today, and trust that we'll find a way to handle the rest together."

With renewed determination, Becca joined the group for the day's tasks. Despite the lingering doubts, she pushed herself to stay present and engaged. As they worked side by side, Sarah and Emma offered constant encouragement, their camaraderie lifting Becca's spirits.

In the afternoon, they received news that the river's water level had stabilized, thanks in large part to their efforts. It was a significant victory, and the group celebrated with a sense of accomplishment and relief.

But just as Becca was starting to feel more confident, a new crisis emerged. One of the local children, a little girl named Mia, had gone missing, and the community was in a state of panic. The youth group immediately sprang into action, organizing search parties to scour the area.

Becca's heart raced as she joined the search. The thought of a child in danger reignited her deepest fears. Her mind flashed back to her own childhood, the paralyzing anxiety that had kept her from participating in so many activities.

As they combed through the dense forest, Becca's fears threatened to consume her. She could feel the familiar tightness in her chest and the growing unease that made it hard to breathe. But then she looked at Sarah and Emma, their determination unwavering, and she drew strength from their resolve.

"We'll find her," Sarah said firmly, her voice cutting through Becca's concern. "We have to."

Hours passed, and the sun began to set, casting long shadows over the forest floor. Just when they were about to regroup, Becca heard a faint cry for help. She froze, straining to listen. There it was again, a child's voice calling out in the distance.

"This way!" Becca shouted, breaking into a run. The others followed, their flashlights piercing the growing darkness. They found Mia huddled under a tree, scared and shivering but unharmed.

Becca felt a wave of relief as they found the little girl. The community's gratitude was evident, and as they returned to camp, Mia's parents thanked them profusely, tears of joy in their eyes.

That night, as the group sat around the campfire, Becca reflected on the day's events. She had faced her fears head-on and emerged stronger for it. The support of her friends and the guidance of Pastor John had been instrumental in helping her navigate the challenges.

But as she lay in her tent, exhaustion finally taking over, a new fear crept into her mind. The journey was far from over, and the next phase of their mission loomed ahead. Becca knew that she would need to confront her deepest fear yet, a fear that had been lurking in the shadows of her mind for years.

The path ahead was uncertain, and the stakes were higher than ever. Becca's resolve would be tested in ways she couldn't yet imagine, and the outcome would depend on her ability to harness the courage she had discovered within herself. The journey was just beginning, and Becca's greatest challenge lay ahead.

The next morning, as the group gathered for breakfast, Becca felt a sense of unease. The previous day's events had shaken her, but she was determined to stay focused. Pastor John had pulled her aside to discuss the upcoming tasks for the day, and Becca was anxious about what lay ahead.

"Becca, there's a significant task that needs to be done today," Pastor John said, his tone serious. "We need someone to lead the team to repair the community center's roof. It's a critical job, and it requires someone with your level of commitment and attention to detail."

Becca's heart skipped a beat. Leading the team was a big responsibility, and the thought of climbing onto a roof filled her with dread. "I don't know if I'm the right person for this," she admitted, her voice trembling.

"You are," Pastor John assured her. "You've shown incredible growth and strength. This is an opportunity for you to take another step forward."

Sarah and Emma, who had been listening nearby, joined the conversation. "We'll help you, Becca," Sarah said, her eyes filled with determination. We're with you every step of the way."

"Absolutely," Emma agreed. "We've faced so much already. Let's get through this together."

Becca took a deep breath, feeling a mixture of fear and determination. "Okay," she said, her voice steadier. "Let's do this."

As the team gathered their tools and supplies, Becca focused on the task ahead. The climb up the ladder was nerve-wracking, to say the least, but with Sarah and Emma's encouragement, she made it up to the roof. The view from the top was both exhilarating and terrifying, but Becca pushed her fears aside and concentrated on the work.

The hours passed quickly as the team worked together, repairing the damaged roof. Becca's confidence grew with each successful task, and she found herself leading the group with a newfound sense of purpose. By the time the sun began to set, the roof was nearly complete, and Becca felt a strong sense of achievement in their accomplishment.

As they descended from the roof, the community members gathered to thank them. Becca felt a deep sense of fulfillment, knowing that their efforts had made a real difference. The gratitude and admiration from the locals were deeply moving, filling Becca's heart with warmth.

That evening, as the group gathered around the campfire, Becca reflected on the day's events. She had confronted her fears and emerged stronger. The support from her friends and the wisdom of Pastor John had played a key role in guiding her through the challenges.

But as the night grew darker, Becca's mind returned to the conversation she had with Pastor John about their next mission. She knew that the journey ahead would be even more challenging, but she felt a renewed sense of determination.

The group sat in a circle, sharing stories and laughter. Becca felt a deep connection with her friends and the community. She realized that she was no longer the scared girl who had arrived at the mission. She had grown into a confident and capable young woman, ready to face whatever challenges lay ahead.

As the fire crackled and the stars twinkled above, she felt a sense of anticipation for the future, knowing that she had the strength and support to overcome any obstacle. The future was uncertain, but Becca felt equipped to face it with courage and determination.

The night was peaceful, but Becca's mind was already turning to the next day. She knew that the mission was just beginning, and she felt a sense of excitement and trepidation for the challenges that lay ahead. The journey was far from over, but Becca was ready to face it with courage and determination.

Chapter 19

The sun began to rise, casting a golden hue over the camp as Becca sat alone by the lake, staring at her reflection in the still water. Today was the day she would confront her deepest fear, and it was not just a personal fear but one directly related to the mission they were on. The task at hand was not just a physical challenge but an emotional one that struck at the core of her fears about her own capabilities.

The previous night, Becca had agreed to take on a task that involved not just physical effort but also a deep personal vulnerability. The local community had asked for help in a part of the mission that involved rebuilding homes, but specifically, they needed volunteers to help organize and facilitate a community event. This event was meant to bring people together to share their experiences and needs, and it required someone to speak publicly and coordinate activities—a task that filled Becca with dread.

Becca had always struggled with public speaking and organizing groups. The thought of standing in front of people, trying to coordinate an event, and speaking about the mission made her heart race. Her fear was not just about speaking but about failing to live up to the expectations of those who depended on her.

Sarah and Emma joined Becca at the lake, their presence a steadying force. "Ready for today?" Sarah asked, her voice warm and encouraging.

Becca took a deep breath, trying to steady her nerves. "I don't know if I can do this," she admitted, her voice trembling. "The idea of speaking in front of everyone and organizing this event . . . it terrifies me."

"You don't have to face this alone," Emma said gently. "We'll be right by your side. It's okay to be scared—what matters is giving it a try, not being perfect."

The three friends walked back to the camp where Pastor John was waiting for them. Becca's stomach was in knots, and she could hardly focus on the words of encouragement he was giving. The thought of facing the community and leading the event loomed over her, creating a sense of terror.

Pastor John noticed Becca's anxiety and approached her with a reassuring smile. "Becca, I know this is a big step, but you've come so far already. You've faced so many fears. This is another opportunity to grow and to make a difference."

Becca nodded, but her mind was racing. "Pastor, can we talk for a moment?" she asked, her voice barely above a whisper.

"Of course," Pastor John said, leading her to a quieter spot. "What's on your mind?"

Becca took a deep breath. "I'm really struggling with this task. The idea of speaking in front of everyone and organizing the event . . . it's my biggest fear. I feel like I'm going to mess up and let everyone down. What if I can't handle it?"

Pastor John listened intently. "Becca, it's natural to feel nervous. But remember, facing our fears is how we grow. You have a team of people here who believe in you. And more importantly, you have shown incredible strength throughout this journey."

"But what if I fail?" Becca asked, her voice cracking.

"Failure is a part of growth," Pastor John said gently. "It's not about being perfect; it's about doing your best and learning from the experience. You've already made a huge impact by being here and by showing up. Let's take it one step at a time."

QUEST FOR COURAGE

Becca felt a flicker of reassurance from Pastor John's words. She knew that with the support of her friends and mentors, she had a chance to overcome this fear. Still, the thought of facing the community and leading the event loomed over her, creating a sense of apprehension.

The day of the event arrived, and Becca felt her nerves intensify as she prepared for the task. The community center was bustling with activity, and Becca's role was to coordinate the various activities and facilitate discussions. The task was terrifying, and her heart raced as she approached the center.

Sarah and Emma were by her side, providing encouragement and support. "We're here with you," Emma said, giving Becca a reassuring smile.

Becca nodded, trying to muster the courage to face the crowd. As she took her position at the front of the room, her hands trembled, and her voice wavered as she began to speak. She introduced herself and briefly explained the purpose of the event. The room was filled with expectant faces, and Becca felt a surge of anxiety.

Despite her fear, Becca pushed through, facilitating discussions and guiding activities. It wasn't easy, and there were moments when she felt she was stumbling, but she kept moving forward, focusing on the task at hand and the support of her friends.

The event went on, and though Becca made mistakes, the community was understanding and appreciative of the effort. As the day drew to a close, Becca felt a mixture of exhaustion and relief. She had faced her fear and done her best, and the feedback from the community was positive.

That evening, as the group gathered around the campfire, Becca reflected on the day's events. She felt a sense of accomplishment, but the fear of failure still lingered. She knew she had made progress, but she also knew there was more work to be done.

Pastor John approached her, with an approving smile. "You did a great job today, Becca. How do you feel?"

Becca took a deep breath. "I'm relieved it's over, but I'm also worried about how I did. What if I didn't do enough?"

"You did more than you think," Pastor John said. "Facing your fear and doing your best is what truly matters. You've shown great courage, and that's truly commendable."

As the night grew darker, Becca felt a sense of peace settling over her. She had confronted her deepest fear and had done her best. But just as she began to relax, a new challenge emerged.

A loud commotion erupted from the direction of the camp's edge. Becca's heart raced as she and her friends rushed to see what had happened. They found a group of people arguing over a miscommunication that had led to a significant issue with the event setup.

Becca's immediate reaction was to freeze, her newfound confidence wavering. The sight of the chaos and the heightened emotions made her anxiety spike. She glanced at Sarah and Emma, who were already working to diffuse the situation.

"Come on, Becca," Sarah urged, her voice steady. "We need your help."

Becca took a deep breath, forcing herself to move. She could feel the weight of the day's events and the new challenge ahead. As she approached the group, she focused on the task at hand, determined to contribute to resolving the issue.

With Sarah and Emma's support, Becca worked to mediate the situation, using her communication skills to address the concerns and find a solution. The argument gradually subsided, and the group began to work together again.

As the campfire crackled in the background, Becca reflected on the day. She had faced her deepest fear and contributed to resolving a new challenge. But she knew that the journey was far from over and that there would be more obstacles to confront.

The sound of footsteps approaching broke her thoughts. She looked up to see Sarah and Emma, their faces illuminated by the firelight. "We wanted to check on you," Sarah said, sitting down beside her.

Becca smiled, feeling a warmth in her heart. "I'm okay," she said. "Actually, I'm better than okay. I'm ready for whatever comes next."

Emma nodded, her eyes reflecting the fire's glow. "That's great to hear. We'll be here to support you through everything that comes your way."

As they sat together, the fire crackling in the background, Becca felt a renewed sense of purpose. She was ready to face her fears and embrace the challenges ahead, knowing that with the support of her friends and mentors, she could conquer anything.

Just as Becca began to feel settled, Pastor John hurried over with a serious expression on his face. "Becca, I need to talk to you about something important."

Becca's heart skipped a beat. "What's wrong?"

Pastor John's face was grave. "There's been a sudden development regarding the area we were helping. There's been a new emergency, and they need urgent assistance. It's a situation that will require immediate action."

Becca's mind raced, her previous confidence fading. "What do we need to do?"

Pastor John handed her a report detailing the new emergency. "We need to assess the situation and decide how we can contribute. It's a significant challenge, and it will test everything we've been working towards."

Becca took the report, her hands trembling. The reality of the new crisis was overwhelming, and she felt a wave of fear crashing over her.

The mission had just taken an unexpected turn, and the challenges ahead were significant.

As Becca stared at the report, she knew that the journey was far from over and that the real test of her growth and courage was just beginning. The next steps would be crucial, and she would need to summon every ounce of strength and resolve she had gained. The weight of the new challenge hung heavily in the air, and Becca faced an uncertain and potentially perilous path ahead.

The campfire's glow flickered in the darkness as Becca prepared for the new obstacles on the horizon.

Chapter 20

The morning sun bathed the camp in a soft, golden light, casting long shadows that danced across the ground. Becca awoke with a renewed sense of purpose, the weight of the recent challenges still fresh in her mind but tempered by a newfound strength. The urgency of the recent emergency and her role in helping the community had ignited a transformation within her, one that was beginning to manifest in her daily life.

Becca stretched, feeling the warmth of the sun on her face as she sat up. She glanced around at the sleeping forms of her friends, Sarah and Emma, and felt a surge of gratitude for their unwavering support. The shadows of her past fears seemed to be melting away, replaced by a steady, growing confidence.

As she joined Sarah and Emma for breakfast, Becca's demeanor had noticeably shifted. There was a calm confidence in her voice and a lightness in her step that hadn't been there before. She was more engaged, more present, and her interactions with her friends reflected her growing self-assurance.

"Morning, Becca!" Sarah greeted cheerfully as Becca approached. "How are you feeling today?"

Becca smiled, a genuine, unburdened smile. "I'm feeling good. Last night was tough, but I'm ready for whatever comes next. It's amazing how much we've grown over the past few weeks."

Emma nodded in agreement, her eyes reflecting the warmth of the morning sun. "We've all come a long way. You've been incredible, Becca. I can see the change in you."

The three friends chatted as they prepared for the day's tasks, which now included final preparations for the remaining days of the mission trip. They were tasked with coordinating a large community event to provide much-needed supplies and support. Becca had taken on a leadership role in organizing the event, and her confidence was evident in the way she handled the arrangements.

The morning was filled with activity as the team worked to finalize details for the event. Becca, Sarah, and Emma organized supplies, coordinated with local volunteers, and ensured that all aspects of the event were in place. Becca's newfound confidence was apparent as she confidently led the team, making decisions and addressing any issues that arose with poise and assurance.

Throughout the day, Becca demonstrated a newfound faith in her abilities. She navigated through the complexities of the event with a sense of calm efficiency, coordinating with local volunteers and ensuring that everything was prepared. The once-daunting task of public speaking and organizing seemed almost natural now, as if the fears that had once held her back had been replaced by a quiet determination.

The community responded positively to their efforts, and the event was shaping up to be a success. Becca's leadership and confidence inspired the rest of the team, and the atmosphere was filled with a sense of camaraderie and purpose.

As the event approached, the group worked tirelessly to ensure everything was prepared. Becca's leadership and confidence inspired the rest of the team, and the atmosphere was filled with a sense of unity and shared purpose. The community was engaged and excited about the upcoming event, and the team's hard work seemed to be paying off.

However, just as everything seemed to be falling into place, an unexpected event threatened to test Becca's newfound faith. That evening, as the team gathered around the campfire to discuss the final details of the event, a local leader approached with urgent news.

"There's been a sudden storm warning," the leader announced, his expression serious. "It's expected to hit tonight, and it could affect the event tomorrow. We need to prepare for the possibility of severe weather and ensure that everything is secured."

The news hit Becca like a cold wave. The storm could jeopardize everything they had worked so hard to achieve. The possibility of the event being canceled or disrupted created a surge of anxiety within her. She glanced at Sarah and Emma, who were already discussing contingency plans, and felt the weight of the situation pressing down on her.

Becca took a deep breath, trying to steady her racing heart. "We need to make sure everyone is safe and that we have a plan in place," she said, her voice steady despite the storm of emotions inside her. "Let's assess the situation and see what we can do."

As the group sprang into action, Becca took charge of coordinating the response to the storm. She worked closely with local volunteers and team members to secure supplies, reinforce structures, and communicate with the community. Her focus was unwavering, and she drew on the strength and faith she had developed throughout the mission trip.

The storm clouds loomed on the horizon as the day drew to a close. Becca and her team worked late into the night, preparing for the worst and hoping for the best. The atmosphere was tense but filled with determination. Becca's leadership and calm demeanor were a source of reassurance for everyone involved.

As the night wore on, the first signs of the storm began to make their presence known. The wind picked up, rustling through the trees and causing the camp's tents to flap ominously. The temperature dropped, and a heavy, oppressive air settled over the camp. Becca and her team continued to work, their breaths visible in the chilly night air.

Becca moved among the volunteers, offering words of encouragement and ensuring that everyone remained focused on their tasks. She coordinated efforts to secure supplies and make last-minute adjustments to the event setup. Her mind was racing with concerns about the storm's potential impact, but she was determined to remain calm and keep the team motivated.

As the first raindrops began to fall, Becca felt a knot of anxiety tighten in her chest. The storm was now an undeniable reality, and its arrival was imminent. She glanced at Sarah and Emma, who were working diligently alongside her. Their presence provided a sense of comfort, and Becca drew strength from their support.

The wind howled as the rain intensified, and the storm's full force bore down on the camp. Becca and her team battled against the elements, securing tents, reinforcing structures, and ensuring that everyone remained safe. The night was a blur of activity and determination, with Becca's leadership guiding the way.

Despite the challenges, Becca remained resolute. She refused to let the storm derail their efforts and focused on maintaining a sense of hope and purpose. Her confidence, built through the trials of the mission trip, was now a beacon for the team.

As the storm raged on, Becca took a moment to step outside and survey the scene. The rain was coming down in torrents, and the wind was howling through the camp. Becca's heart was pounding, but she took a deep breath and reminded herself of the progress they had made.

In the midst of the storm, Becca's thoughts turned to the impact of their mission. She thought about the community they were helping, the lives they were touching, and the difference they were making. The storm was a test, but it was also an opportunity to prove their resilience and commitment.

As the first light of dawn began to break through the storm clouds, Becca felt a sense of cautious optimism. The worst of the storm seemed to have passed, and the team's efforts had paid off. The event was still on track, and Becca's leadership had played a crucial role in navigating the challenges.

The storm's aftermath left the camp in a state of disarray, but Becca and her team were determined to persevere. They worked tirelessly to assess the damage, make repairs, and ensure that everything was ready for the event.

With the storm behind them, Becca felt a renewed sense of determination. The challenges they had faced had strengthened her resolve and deepened her commitment to the mission. She knew that the final days of the trip would be critical, and she was prepared to face whatever came next.

As the sun rose higher in the sky, Becca took a moment to reflect on the journey. The storm had tested her faith and her leadership, but it had also revealed her inner strength and resilience. She was ready to continue the mission, knowing that the journey was far from over and that there were still many challenges and opportunities ahead.

Chapter 21

As the days in the affected town stretched on, the mission team faced a series of big tasks. The work was grueling, and the exhaustion was noticeable, but the group's spirit remained high, driven by their sense of purpose and the support they offered one another.

Finally, the situation in the town began to stabilize. Becca, Sarah, and Emma were worn out but pleased of their efforts. They had risen to the occasion, proving their resilience and commitment. The group's departure was set for the following morning, and anticipation of returning home was mixed with a sense of unfinished business.

That evening, as they prepared for their final night in the town, Pastor John gathered the team around the campfire. The flames cast a warm glow, providing a stark contrast to the fatigue etched on everyone's faces. The campfire had become their place for reflection, and tonight was no different.

"We've done remarkable work here," Pastor John began, his voice steady but tired. "Your dedication and hard work have made a significant impact on this community. Tomorrow, we'll head back home, but before we do, I have some important news to share."

The group leaned in, curiosity piqued. Becca's thoughts drifted to the complexities of their mission and the unresolved aspects of their journey. She hoped for a smooth conclusion to their trip and the chance to return to a sense of normalcy.

Pastor John continued, "I've been in touch with the school regarding your concerns about missing so much in your classes. They've reviewed your situation and sent an email today with their decision."

Becca's heart skipped a beat. Her anxiety over the missed school days had been a persistent shadow, and the uncertainty of how it would affect her future weighed heavily on her.

Pastor John pulled out his phone and read aloud from the email. "The school has acknowledged the importance of the work you've done. They're willing to offer you an extended deadline for your assignments and make accommodations for the time you've missed. They're impressed by your dedication and the positive impact you've made. However, there will be a few requirements for you to meet upon your return, including additional assignments and a review of the material covered during your absence."

A wave of relief washed over Becca. The school's understanding and flexibility were a huge relief, and the pressure of falling behind had lifted somewhat. She glanced at Sarah and Emma, who also showed signs of relief. The weight of their missed school days was finally beginning to ease.

Pastor John smiled at the group. "I know this news is a huge relief. You've all worked incredibly hard, and it's clear that your efforts have made a real difference. As we head back tomorrow, let's carry this sense of accomplishment with us and remember the impact we've had."

The group nodded in agreement, their spirits buoyed by the news. The journey home seemed a bit lighter, and the upcoming challenges felt more manageable. They shared stories around the campfire, their conversations a mix of nostalgia for their work and anticipation for their return.

As the night deepened, Becca felt a mix of exhaustion and satisfaction. The mission had been more challenging than she had imagined, but it had also been a profound learning experience. She looked forward to returning home, but her mind lingered on the journey ahead and the adjustments that awaited her.

The following morning, as they prepared to leave, the mood was a blend of excitement and fatigue. The team packed up their gear and said their goodbyes to the community they had helped. The journey back was filled with reflections on their accomplishments and the challenges they had faced.

Becca sat quietly, reflecting on the growth she had experienced. The support from her friends, the guidance from Pastor John, and the strength she had found within herself were sources of pride. Yet, there was a lingering sense of apprehension about what awaited them back home.

As the bus pulled away from the town, Becca looked out the window, taking in the final views of the place that had become a significant part of their journey. The road ahead was unknown, but the experiences they had shared had forged a stronger bond among them.

The bus ride was filled with a mix of conversations, laughter, and quiet contemplation. Becca knew that their return home would bring its own set of challenges, but she felt better equipped to handle them. The mission had been a transformative experience, and the lessons that she had learned would stay with her for a lifetime.

Conversations on the bus bubbled up as team members began to reflect on their experiences. Sarah and Emma sat across from Becca, their tired faces illuminated by the soft glow of the bus lights.

"I can't believe we're heading home already," Sarah said, her voice tinged with both relief and nostalgia. "It feels like we've been here forever, and at the same time, no time at all."

Becca nodded, feeling a similar sense of disbelief. "I know. This place has become so familiar, and leaving feels bittersweet. But at the same time, I'm really surprised with how much we accomplished."

Emma, who had been quiet for a while, spoke up. "I'm glad we were able to help so many people. I never imagined I'd feel this close to everyone on the team. It's been an amazing experience."

The conversation turned to lighter topics as the bus rolled along. Stories about the funny moments and small victories during the mission sparked laughter among the group. Emma recounted a particularly amusing incident involving a miscommunication with a local child, prompting chuckles from everyone.

As the night wore on, the group began to settle into a more reflective mood. Pastor John sat at the front of the bus, looking thoughtful as he gazed out the window. He had been a steady presence throughout the trip, guiding and supporting the team.

Becca leaned forward to catch his eye. "Pastor John, I wanted to thank you again for everything. The email from the school really took a load off my mind. It means a lot to me."

Pastor John smiled warmly. "You all worked incredibly hard, and you've made a real difference here. I'm glad the school was able to accommodate you. It's a testament to the impact you've had."

Sarah joined the conversation, her voice filled with gratitude. "Yeah, and thank you for being so understanding about everything. I was worried about the impact on our grades, too."

Pastor John nodded. "It's important to balance your responsibilities, and I'm proud of how you've handled everything. Remember, though, that the experiences you've gained here are just as valuable as any academic achievement."

The bus continued its journey, the rhythmic hum of the engine lulling some to sleep. Becca found herself lost in thought, reflecting on the transformation she had undergone. The mission had pushed her beyond her comfort zone, and she felt a newfound sense of confidence and purpose.

As dawn approached, the bus neared their hometown. The familiar sights of their community began to emerge on the horizon. Becca's thoughts were a swirl of anticipation and concern. She was eager to return home, but she also felt a lingering sense of uncertainty about how the changes in her would be received.

Sarah and Emma were still chatting animatedly, their excitement about returning home evident. Becca appreciated their enthusiasm but found herself wondering about the challenges that lay ahead. She hoped to carry forward the lessons she had learned and apply them to her daily life, but she knew it wasn't going to be easy.

The bus pulled into the parking lot of the church, their final destination. Families and friends were waiting for their arrival, eager to welcome them back. Becca spotted her parents and younger brother, Jason, standing near the entrance. Her mom's eyes were filled with relief and pride, and Jason waved enthusiastically.

As Becca disembarked, she was enveloped in a warm hug from her mom. "Welcome home, Becca! We're so glad you got home safely. We missed you so much."

Becca smiled, feeling a mix of relief and nervousness. "Thanks, Mom. It's good to be home."

Pastor John gathered the team for a final debriefing. "Before you all head off to your families, I want to let you know that the school has sent another update. They've acknowledged the impact of your work and have offered additional support to help you transition back into your studies."

Becca's heart lifted at the news. The school's continued support was a reassuring sign that her efforts were recognized and valued. As she looked around at her friends and fellow team members, she felt a deep sense of gratitude for the journey they had shared.

The team began to say their goodbyes and reconnect with their families. Becca's thoughts turned to the future and the challenges she would face as she reintegrated into her routine. The mission had been a transformative experience, but the real test would be applying the lessons learned to her everyday life.

As the day progressed, Becca and her family settled back into their home. The comfort of familiar surroundings was a stark contrast to the intensity of the mission, and Becca felt a sense of both relief and unease. She was eager to reconnect with her friends and continue her journey, but she knew that the impact of the mission would continue to resonate within her.

The chapter of their mission trip had closed, but the story of Becca's transformation was just beginning. As she prepared to face the challenges of returning to school and adjusting to life back home, she carried with her the strength and resilience she had discovered along the way.

With the support of her friends, family, and Pastor John, Becca felt ready to tackle the new chapter of her life. The journey home had marked the end of one adventure and the beginning of another, and Becca was determined to embrace the future with courage and confidence.

Chapter 22

The early morning light filtered gently through Becca's bedroom window, casting long shadows across the room. The day after their return was a quiet one, filled with the simple rhythms of reestablishing normalcy. Becca moved through her home, reacquainting herself with the everyday comforts that had seemed so distant during their mission trip.

As she walked into the kitchen, she found Jason already at the table, eating his breakfast. His eyes widened as he took in the changes in his sister. "You seem different," he said, a mix of curiosity and admiration in his voice. Becca smiled, ruffling his hair affectionately. "I've learned a lot, Jay. It's hard to explain, but I feel . . . stronger."

Jason's eyes sparkled with interest. "Really? What did you learn?"

Becca hesitated, searching for the right words. "I think I've learned that facing fears can change everything. I'm more confident now. I think I can handle things better."

Jason nodded thoughtfully, clearly impressed by her newfound maturity. "That's cool. I've seen you work through stuff and it's like you're a superhero now."

Becca chuckled, "Not quite a superhero, but I've certainly grown."

The house was abuzz with a feeling of normalcy, yet Becca's mind was still replaying the events of the mission trip. The comforts of home felt soothing, yet they also seemed to contrast sharply with the intensity of her recent experiences. Her parents were relieved to have their daughter back, even though they had not been able to join the mission trip themselves. They were supportive and eager to hear about her adventures, though Becca sensed a mixture of concern and curiosity in their eyes.

Monday morning brought the challenge of reintegrating into daily life and school. The familiar routine seemed both comforting and unsettling. As Becca walked through the school hallways, she was greeted with friendly nods and curious glances. Her friends were eager to hear about her trip, and Becca found herself recounting the experiences with a new sense of excitement and accomplishment.

In her classes, Becca's mind occasionally wandered back to the mission trip. The lessons she had learned about courage, faith, and community were now deeply embedded in her thoughts. She found herself more engaged in her schoolwork, driven by a newfound motivation to apply what she had learned.

Her interactions with friends and teachers were more confident, and she approached each day with a renewed sense of purpose. The fears that had once seemed insurmountable now felt manageable, thanks to the support and growth she had experienced during the trip. However, the reality of the increased homework load began to set in. Becca realized that she had missed quite a bit of schoolwork, and catching up would not be easy.

Wednesday evening, as Becca and her family prepared for the upcoming church service, Becca received a message from Pastor John. The church had been buzzing with excitement about the upcoming opportunities for the youth group. The message hinted at a new initiative that involved the youth group, but it wasn't specific about the details.

Becca's curiosity was piqued as she discussed the message with Sarah and Emma, who had also received the same information. They shared their excitement and speculation about the new initiative. The possibility of a new project or mission filled Becca with a mixture of anticipation and apprehension. However, Becca couldn't ignore the practical concerns that were creeping in. "Do you think it's a good idea to start another project so soon? We just got back and our homework is doubled because of all the time we took off."

Sarah nodded, her own expression a mix of excitement and concern. "Yeah, it's a lot. I'm already feeling the pressure to catch up."

Emma chimed in, "Maybe we can talk to Pastor John about it. He might understand our situation better than we think."

As they arrived at the church that evening, the vibrant atmosphere was alive with energy. Pastor John greeted them warmly, and after a brief introduction, he gathered the youth group for a special announcement.

"We have a new opportunity coming up for you all," Pastor John began, his eyes sparkling with enthusiasm. "It's something that will challenge you, but also allow you to make a significant impact. I'll share more details soon, but I wanted you all to know that this is going to be an exciting next step for us."

The room buzzed with excited chatter as Becca glanced around at her friends. The excitement was evident, but so was the uncertainty. As the group dispersed, Becca felt a familiar flutter of anxiety mixed with eagerness. This new opportunity was a chance to continue growing and applying the lessons she had learned, but it also represented a new challenge.

After the meeting, Becca approached Pastor John. "Pastor, do you have a minute?"

"Of course, Becca. What's on your mind?"

She took a deep breath, "We're all excited about the new initiative, but we just got back and we have an awful lot of homework to catch up on. I'm worried about balancing everything."

Pastor John nodded thoughtfully. "I understand your concerns, Becca. Balancing school and these projects is important. Let me talk to the school on your behalf and see if we can work something out. You're not alone. Others have mentioned the same thing to me."

Becca felt a wave of relief wash over her. "Thank you, Pastor. That means a lot."

As Becca headed home, she couldn't shake the feeling that this new opportunity might bring another test of her courage and faith. She was eager to see what lay ahead but also wary of what challenges it might bring.

Her phone buzzed with a notification, and she saw a reminder from Pastor John about an upcoming meeting to discuss the new initiative. The anticipation of what was to come made her both excited and cautious. The road ahead was uncertain, but Becca felt a renewed sense of purpose and readiness to face whatever came next.

The new opportunity at church loomed on the horizon, promising to bring further growth and transformation. As Becca looked ahead to the next chapter of her journey, she realized that her experiences had only begun to influence her future.

Chapter 23

As Becca settled back into her routine, she found herself more involved in the new church activities. The announcement of the new initiative had brought a wave of excitement and anticipation, and Becca was eager to be a part of it. The first meeting to discuss the details was scheduled for the following weekend, and Becca, Sarah, and Emma made sure to be there.

The church was abuzz with energy when they arrived. The youth group gathered in the community hall, where Pastor John stood at the front, ready to share more about the new initiative.

"Welcome, everyone," Pastor John began, smiling warmly at the group. "I'm thrilled to see so many of you here. This new initiative is a community outreach program designed to help those in need right here in our city. We'll be organizing various events, from food drives to after-school tutoring programs. It's a fantastic opportunity to make a difference and to grow together as a group."

Becca felt a surge of excitement. She had always wanted to contribute more to her community, and this seemed like the perfect opportunity. As the meeting progressed, they were divided into smaller teams, each focusing on a different aspect of the initiative. Becca, Sarah, and Emma found themselves in the same team, assigned to organize a community event to raise awareness and gather resources for local families in need.

The next few weeks were a whirlwind of activity. Becca and her friends spent their afternoons planning the event, brainstorming ideas, and coordinating with other team members. The church hall became their second home as they worked late into the evenings, driven by a shared sense of purpose and excitement.

However, amidst the excitement, the girls couldn't ignore their mounting schoolwork. The extra workload from missed classes during the mission trip was starting to pile up, causing them significant stress. One evening, as they wrapped up their meeting, Becca voiced her concerns.

"Guys, I'm really worried about all the schoolwork we've missed," Becca said, her brows furrowed with anxiety. "I don't want to fall behind."

Sarah nodded, her face mirroring Becca's concern. "Yeah, I've been thinking about that too. Maybe we should talk to Pastor John and see if we can focus our efforts on weekends. That way, we can keep up with our schoolwork during the week."

Emma agreed, adding, "I think that's a good idea. We need to find a balance."

The next day, the girls approached Pastor John with their concerns. He listened attentively, his face thoughtful.

"Your education is important, and I don't want this initiative to interfere with your schoolwork," Pastor John said kindly. "Why don't we adjust your schedules so you can focus on these activities during the weekends? That way, you'll have the weekdays free for your studies."

The girls breathed a collective sigh of relief. "That would be amazing, Pastor John," Becca said, grateful for his understanding.

As the event date approached, Becca's role within the youth group grew more prominent. She found herself taking on more responsibilities, coordinating with other teams, and even leading some of the planning sessions. Her confidence had blossomed, and she was no longer the timid girl who had joined the youth group months ago.

The day of the event finally arrived. The church hall was transformed into a bustling hub of activity, with booths, games, and information tables set up for the community. Becca's heart swelled with a sense of accomplishment as she looked around at what they had achieved. Families began to arrive, and the atmosphere was filled with laughter and excitement.

As Becca moved through the crowd, helping where she could, she felt a tap on her shoulder. She turned to see Pastor John, a proud smile on his face.

"Becca, you've done an incredible job," he said. "I admire the way you've grown and all that you've achieved. There's something I'd like to ask you."

Becca's curiosity was piqued. "What is it, Pastor?"

"We have a special presentation later today, and I'd like you to speak about your experiences and the journey you've been on with the youth group. I think your story would inspire a lot of people."

Becca's heart skipped a beat. Public speaking had always been one of her greatest fears. The thought of standing in front of a crowd and sharing her story made her stomach churn. But as she looked around at the faces of her friends, the people she had grown so close to, and the community they were helping, she felt a flicker of courage.

"I . . . I'll do it," she said, her voice trembling slightly. "I'll share my story."

Pastor John's smile widened. "I knew you would. You're stronger than you realize, Becca."

As the time for the presentation drew near, Becca felt a mix of excitement and fear. She had come so far, and now she had the chance to inspire others with her journey. She took a deep breath, remembering the support of her friends and the lessons she had learned.

The moment arrived, and Becca stepped up to the podium. The room fell silent as she began to speak, her voice shaky at first but growing stronger with each word. She shared her fears, her struggles, and the incredible journey of growth and courage she had experienced.

As she spoke, she saw nods of understanding and smiles of encouragement from the audience.

When she finished, the room erupted in applause. Becca felt a surge of relief and a sense of connection with the people around her. She had faced her fear head on and conquered it, and in doing so, she had taken another step forward in her journey of faith and courage.

As the applause died down, Becca caught sight of Pastor John's approving nod and the encouraging smiles of Sarah and Emma. She understood that this was merely the start. Though many challenges lay ahead, she felt prepared to confront them, bolstered by her friends' support and her newfound confidence.

The excitement of the day was capped off by an announcement from Pastor John. "Before we conclude," he said, "I'd like to share some wonderful news. Our church has been given the opportunity to partner with a local organization for an extended outreach program. This will give us a chance to make an even bigger impact in our community."

The room buzzed with excitement, but Becca couldn't help but feel a pang of anxiety. The thought of taking on even more responsibility, especially with their school workload, was troublesome.

As they left the event, Becca, Sarah, and Emma walked together, discussing the new initiative. "Do you think we can handle this with all our schoolwork?" Sarah asked, voicing the concern that was on all their minds.

Becca nodded slowly. "It's going to be a lot, but maybe we can manage it if we stick to weekends and really plan our time well."

Emma smiled, her confidence bolstering the group. "Together, we can face anything that comes our way."

Despite their reassurances, Becca couldn't shake the feeling of doubt. The balance between their commitments was delicate, and she knew it would take all their effort to maintain it. But as she looked at her friends, she felt a renewed sense of determination. They had faced challenges before and come out stronger. This would be no different.

As they walked out of the church, they ran into Pastor John, who was talking to a group of parents. He waved them over, a smile spreading across his face. "I wanted to let you girls know that I've spoken with the school about your concerns. They're willing to work with us on this. They understand the importance of what you're doing and are supportive of your efforts."

Becca felt a wave of relief wash over her. "Thank you, Pastor John. That's great!"

Pastor John nodded. "You've all shown incredible dedication and growth. I have no doubt that you'll continue to thrive, both in your schoolwork and in your service to the community."

As they walked home, Becca couldn't help but feel a sense of excitement for the future. The new opportunity was a chance to keep evolving, discovering, and making an impact.

As they reached Becca's house, her phone buzzed with a notification. She glanced at it and saw an email from an unknown sender. Opening it, she read the subject line: "Urgent: A New Opportunity Awaits." Becca's heart raced as she clicked on the message, wondering what new challenge lay ahead.

Chapter 24

Becca stared at her phone, her thumb hovering over the screen. The subject line of the new email was impossible to ignore: "Urgent: A New Opportunity Awaits." With a touch of nervous anticipation, she opened it.The message from Pastor John read:

Dear Becca,

I hope this message finds you well. I have an exciting but urgent opportunity that I believe you are perfectly suited for. Our church has been invited to participate in a community conference, and I would like you to be one of the speakers. Your journey and transformation are incredibly inspiring, and I believe your story could make a significant impact on others.

Please let me know if you are interested. We can discuss the details at your earliest convenience.

Blessings,

Pastor John

Becca's pulse quickened. The idea of speaking in front of a large audience was frightening. She had spoken recently at a smaller youth group gathering, where she had shared her experiences with a close-knit audience. Although the event had been less intimidating than she had feared, the prospect of addressing a larger, more diverse group was another challenge entirely.

With a shaky breath, she dialed Pastor John's number. His reassuring voice, though calm and supportive, did little to help her.

"Hi, Pastor John. I saw your email. It sounds like an incredible opportunity, but I'm not sure if I can handle such a big event," Becca said, her voice trembling.

"Becca, I know how scary this can seem. But I've seen how much you've grown since speaking at the youth group event. You were able to connect with that smaller audience and share your story with honesty and courage. This larger event is a chance to reach even more people," Pastor John replied, his tone encouraging.

"I'll need to think about it and talk to my friends," Becca said, her resolve slightly firmer but still uncertain.

Later that afternoon, Becca met Sarah and Emma at their favorite coffee shop. She relayed the details of the email, her anxiety evident in the way she fidgeted with her cup of hot chocolate.

"Pastor John wants me to speak at a community conference. I've never spoken at such a large group before. I'm really scared," Becca confessed.

Sarah, ever supportive, reached across the table and gently placed her hand on Becca's. "You did great before. Yes, you were nervous, but you shared your story with such sincerity. This is just another step forward. We believe in you."

Emma, who had her own history of overcoming fears, nodded in agreement. "We're here for you. How about if we help you prepare. Think of it as a chance to inspire even more people with your story."

Encouraged by her friends' support, Becca felt a flicker of determination. "Alright, I'll do it. Can we start working on it together?"

The weeks leading up to the event were filled with intense preparation. Becca spent hours drafting, refining, and rehearsing her speech. She practiced in front of a mirror, then in front of Sarah and Emma. Her younger brother, Jason, watched her rehearsals with wide eyes, admiring his sister's bravery.

One evening, her mother sat beside her during a practice session. "Becca, we're really impressed with how far you've come. I can see the hard work you've put in, and it's clear you're showing real courage."

Becca nodded, appreciating her family's support but still feeling a knot of anxiety. "Thanks, Mom. I just hope I can help make a difference."

On the day of the conference, Becca arrived at the community center with a mixture of excitement and nervousness. The large hall was filled with lots of people, their chatter buzzing in the background. The bright stage lights made the room feel even more intimidating. Pastor John greeted her with a warm, encouraging smile.

"Becca, you're going to do great. Just speak from your heart. Remember, your story is powerful, and it can make a real difference."

Becca took a deep breath and walked onto the stage. The lights were blinding, and her heart was pounding. She saw Sarah and Emma in the front row, their supportive faces a source of real comfort.

"Hello, everyone. My name is Becca," she began, her voice trembling slightly. "I'm here to share my story with you. A few months ago, I was living in deep fear, afraid to step out of my comfort zone. But with the support of my friends, my family, and my church, I have learned to face my fears and embrace new challenges."

At first, her voice quivered, but as she spoke, she gained confidence. She shared the highs and lows of her journey, including the mission trip, and the lessons she had learned about courage, faith, and friendship. The audience listened attentively, and Becca found strength in their engagement.

As she concluded her speech, the room filled with applause. Becca felt a profound sense of relief and fulfillment. She had faced one of her greatest fears and shared her story with others. The applause was not just for her, but it was a testament to the support she had received from everyone around her.

After the event, Pastor John approached her with a big smile. "You did an amazing job, Becca. You did an amazing job."

Becca returned his smile, feeling a deep sense of gratitude. "Thank you, Pastor John. I couldn't have done this without the support of everyone."

As Becca left the community center, a sense of liberation washed over her. She had taken a significant step forward in her journey of faith and courage. However, as she checked her phone one last time, a new message flashed on the screen, its subject line reading: "A New Opportunity for Growth."

Becca's heart raced as she clicked on the message. What new challenge awaited her? She felt a blend of excitement and curiosity as she wondered about the impact this new opportunity might hold for her future.

Chapter 25

As Becca read the new message titled "A New Opportunity for Growth," her heart raced with a mix of excitement and trepidation. The email outlined a new leadership initiative at school, aiming to develop public speaking skills and lead community projects. The program was designed for students ready to take on significant challenges and lead by example. Becca was intrigued but also hesitant by the thought of adding another commitment to her plate that is already so full.

Feeling unsure, she decided to meet up with Sarah and Emma to discuss the opportunity. They had planned to catch up at their favorite coffee shop, a cozy spot with warm lighting and the comforting scent of freshly brewed coffee.

Becca arrived at the coffee shop just as the late afternoon sun cast a golden glow over the city. Inside, the shop was bustling with patrons, the soft hum of conversation blending in with the clinking of cups. Sarah and Emma were already settled at their usual corner table, a steaming cup of hot cocoa in front of each of them.

"Hey, Becca!" Sarah greeted her with a bright smile as she slid into a seat. "We've been waiting for you. What's this new opportunity you were talking about?"

Becca set her phone down on the table, her fingers tracing the rim of her coffee cup. "It's a leadership program at school. They want us to work on public speaking and community projects. It's a great chance, but honestly, I'm feeling swamped along with everything else."

Emma sipped her hot chocolate thoughtfully. "That does sound intense, especially with the extra schoolwork we have now. What do you think it involves?"

"It's a big commitment," Becca explained, her brow furrowed. "There will be a lot of speaking engagements and leading projects. I'm worried about balancing it with school and other responsibilities. I don't want to take on too much and fall behind."

Sarah reached out and squeezed Becca's hand. "You've already faced so many fears and grown so much. This could be another step in your journey. Remember how you felt about speaking at the smaller group event and then at the conference? You were nervous but handled it so well."

Emma nodded in agreement. "If you decide to take on this new challenge, we can support each other. Maybe we can remind Pastor John about working just on weekends. That way, we can manage both our schoolwork and this new commitment."

Becca's eyes brightened with the idea. "Good idea. I'll talk to Pastor John about it and see if there's a way to adjust our involvements to fit better with our school schedules."

Their conversation continued, filled with reassurances and plans for how they could tackle this new opportunity together. Becca felt a weight lift off her shoulders, comforted by the support from her friends. They spent the rest of their time chatting about their plans and laughing over coffee, which eased Becca's anxiety.

Later that evening, Becca shared her thoughts with her parents. They were gathered in the living room, the warmth of the fire adding to the coziness of their home. Becca's mom was curled up with a book, while her dad was reviewing some work papers.

"How was your meeting with Sarah and Emma?" her mom asked, glancing up with a curious expression.

"It was good," Becca said, sinking into an armchair. "We talked about the new leadership program at school. It's a big opportunity, but I'm worried about how to manage it all."

Her dad put down his papers and looked at her thoughtfully. "It sounds like you're really considering this seriously. What do you think? Do you feel ready for another challenge?"

"I'm not sure," Becca admitted. "It sounds like something I'd like to do, but I'm worried about falling behind with school work. I want to make sure I can handle everything without getting overwhelmed."

Her mom reached out and patted Becca's hand. "It's perfectly okay to feel that way. You've grown so much, and you have the support of your friends and family. Just remember to take it one step at a time and find a balance that works for you."

Becca nodded, feeling reassured by their support. "Thanks. I'll see if I can make it work."

The next morning at school, Becca was reminded of the project when Mrs. Adams, her teacher, made an announcement about it. Becca sat in her seat, listening to the details with a flutter of nerves. The project involved organizing a significant community event and giving presentations—tasks that sounded both exciting and challenging.

As the class ended and students began to chat about the project, Becca felt a pang of uneasiness. She slipped out of the classroom and found a quiet corner in the hallway. Whispering to herself, she closed her eyes and prayed softly, "Are you telling me to do this, Lord?"

The response was almost immediate. A profound sense of calm washed over her, easing the tight knot of worry in her chest. Becca took a deep breath, feeling a newfound clarity about the challenge ahead. She walked back to her classroom with a renewed sense of purpose.

During her lunch break, she caught up with Sarah and Emma to share her decision. They were excited and supportive, discussing the next steps and how they could adjust their schedules to help Becca with the new project.

As Becca prepared for the upcoming project, she felt a sense of peace about the path she was on. With the encouragement from her friends and family, and her own growing confidence, she was ready to embrace this new opportunity and face whatever challenges it might bring.

Chapter 26

The next day, Becca walked into school with a mix of excitement and nervousness. The leadership program was starting, and she was eager to see how she could apply her newfound confidence and faith to this new challenge. As she walked through the hallways, she spotted Sarah and Emma waiting for her by their lockers.

"Ready for the big day?" Sarah asked with a grin.

Becca nodded, her stomach fluttering with anticipation. "Yeah, I think so. I just hope I can handle it."

Emma gave her a reassuring smile. "You can handle this, Becca. We'll be there to support you all the way."

Their first task was to meet with the other students participating in the program. The group gathered in the school auditorium, where the program coordinator, Mrs. Thompson, gave an overview of the upcoming projects and events. Becca listened intently, taking notes and absorbing as much information as she could.

"Each of you will be responsible for leading a team to organize a community event," Mrs. Thompson explained. "This is your chance to make a real impact and develop your leadership skills. "Remember, you are not doing this alone. This is a team effort, so rely on each other for support."

After the meeting, Becca, Sarah, and Emma sat together in the cafeteria, discussing their ideas for the community event. Becca felt a surge of inspiration as they brainstormed, her mind buzzing with possibilities.

"We could organize a charity drive," Sarah suggested. "Maybe collect donations for the local shelter?"

"That's a great idea," Becca agreed. "We could also set up a booth at the school fair to raise awareness and gather more support."

Emma nodded enthusiastically. "I love it! And we can reach out to local businesses for sponsorships. This could really make a difference."

As they continued to plan, Becca felt a growing sense of confidence. The support from her friends was invaluable, and she was determined to make this project a success. They divided up the tasks, with each of them taking on different responsibilities to ensure everything ran smoothly.

Over the next few weeks, Becca faced numerous challenges as they worked on the project. There were moments of doubt and frustration, but she drew strength from her experiences on the mission trip and the lessons she had learned. Whenever she felt like she was over her head, she reminded herself of the importance of faith and perseverance.

One afternoon, while they were setting up for a fundraising event, Becca encountered a significant obstacle. The weather forecast predicted heavy rain, which threatened to derail their plans. Panic set in as she considered the possibility of their hard work going to waste.

"We can't control the weather," Sarah said, trying to stay positive. "But we can come up with a backup plan."

Emma nodded in agreement. "Let's move the event indoors. We can set up in the gym and still have everything we need."

Becca took a deep breath, grateful for their quick thinking. "Okay, let's do it. We'll make this work, no matter what."

With the help of their classmates, they quickly relocated the event into the school gym. Despite the last-minute change, the turnout was incredible. Students, teachers, and community members came together to support the cause, and the event was a resounding success.

As the evening came to a close, Becca stood on the stage, looking out at the crowd. She felt a deep sense of accomplishment and gratitude. As she scanned the faces, she noticed Pastor John standing at the back, an encouraging smile on his face. The challenges they had faced only made their success even sweeter.

After the event, Mrs. Thompson approached Becca with a warm smile. "You did an amazing job, Becca. Your leadership and determination really shone through."

"Thank you, Mrs. Thompson," Becca replied, her heart swelling with gratitude. "I couldn't have done it without Sarah and Emma. We make a great team."

Later that night, as Becca reflected on the day's events, she felt a renewed sense of confidence in her abilities. The experience had reinforced her belief in the power of faith, friendship, and perseverance. She knew that she could face any challenge that came her way.

The next morning, Becca, Sarah, and Emma met up at their favorite coffee shop. The cozy atmosphere and the familiar smell of freshly brewed coffee always made them feel at ease.

"So, what's next for us?" Emma asked, taking a sip of her latte.

Becca smiled. "I guess we just keep applying what we've learned. It's not just about one event; it's about carrying this confidence and faith into everything we do."

Sarah nodded. "And supporting each other, like we always have."

Their conversation was interrupted by the arrival of an email notification on Becca's phone. She quickly checked it and her eyes widened.

"It's from Mrs. Thompson," she said, her voice tinged with curiosity. "She wants to meet with us tomorrow morning. It's about another project."

Emma raised an eyebrow. "Another project? Already?"

Sarah chuckled. "I guess we're becoming the go-to team for these things."

Becca felt a mix of excitement and concern. "I just hope it's not too much. We still have a lot of schoolwork to do with finals coming up and graduation just around the corner."

Emma leaned in, her expression serious. "We'll make it work, Becca. We can talk to Mrs. Thompson and explain our situation. Maybe we can find a way to balance everything."

The next day, the girls met with Mrs. Thompson. She listened to their concerns about their school workload and nodded understandingly.

"I appreciate your honesty," Mrs. Thompson said. "It's important to maintain a balance. How about this: you can focus on the new project during weekends, leaving after school hours for study. That way, you can still keep up with your studies."

Becca felt a wave of relief wash over her. "Thank you, Mrs. Thompson. We'll do our best."

As they left the meeting, Becca felt a sense of peace and clarity. With her friends beside her and her faith guiding her, she felt prepared to tackle whatever challenge may arise.

Later that evening, Becca and her parents sat down for dinner. Jason, who had noticed the changes in Becca since her return, was eager to hear about her day.

"How was school?" he asked, his eyes wide with curiosity.

"It was good," Becca replied with a smile. "We're working on a new project for the leadership program."

Jason's face lit up. "That's awesome! I bet you're going to do great."

Becca's father looked at her with admiration. "You've come a long way, Becca. We're truly amazed with your progress."

"Thanks, Dad," Becca said, feeling a warm glow inside. "It's been a quite a journey, but I'm grateful for everything I've learned and for the support from my friends and family."

Just as she was about to take another bite of her dinner, her phone buzzed with a new message. She glanced at the screen and saw the subject line: 'A New Opportunity for Growth.' Her heart raced as she clicked on the message. And then there was another from the school, titled 'Exciting Mentorship Program Opportunity.' Now what's was this all about?

Chapter 27

Becca's mind buzzed with the implications of the two emails she had received. The first was from Pastor John, outlining a new leadership initiative at the church. The second was from the school, offering a mentorship opportunity for upperclassmen to guide freshmen. Both messages arrived on the heels of a demanding week, leaving Becca both excited and apprehensive about the possibilities ahead.

Later that day, Becca, Sarah, and Emma gathered at their favorite coffee shop, each nursing a warm drink. The cozy atmosphere of their usual spot was a welcome comfort, and the chatter around them created a sense of normalcy. As they settled into their booth, Becca pulled out her phone to share the news.

"Did you both get the emails?" Becca asked, her voice a mix of curiosity and concern.

Sarah nodded, her expression thoughtful. "Yes, I saw them. The school's mentorship program could be a great chance for us to give back, but it's a big responsibility. And the church leadership initiative is appealing, but I'm worried about our capacity to handle both."

Emma sipped her cocoa, her gaze drifting to the window. "I feel the same. We've been so focused on getting through the end of the school year and managing the workload after the mission trip. Diving into something like this just might be too much."

Becca leaned forward, her fingers tracing the rim of her cup. "I agree. While these opportunities are exciting, they also come with a lot of responsibility. We've never done anything like this before, and it's crucial that we be honest about our readiness."

Sarah looked between Becca and Emma, nodding in agreement. "Maybe we should talk to Pastor John about it. We might be better off participating rather than leading, especially since we need more experience in areas like resume building and financial management."

Emma smiled, clearly relieved by the suggestion. "That sounds like a good plan. We can still be involved, but in a way that fits our current capabilities and allows us to learn and grow."

The girls spent the next hour discussing their options and formulating a plan. They agreed to approach Pastor John and express their willingness to support the initiatives but with the caveat that they would need guidance and experience before taking on a leadership role. They were enthusiastic about the mentorship program at school but were unsure about leading the church project due to their lack of experience with resume building and other related tasks.

Becca felt a sense of relief as they wrapped up their discussion. "I'll send a text to Pastor John tonight, letting him know how we're feeling about the leadership initiative. We should also be clear about our interest in the school's mentorship program but need to make sure we can manage it along with our current workload."

Sarah and Emma agreed, and as they finished their coffees, they chatted about the various aspects of the upcoming opportunities. Their conversation was filled with a mix of excitement and apprehension, reflecting their desire to contribute meaningfully while also balancing their existing commitments.

Back at home later that evening, Becca felt a twinge of nervousness as she settled into her room. She decided to check her email one last time before bed. The new message from the school administration caught her eye: "Important Update: Upcoming School Challenge."

With a deep breath, Becca opened the email. The school was organizing a "Spirit Week," which would include a series of fun, simple activities: a themed dress up day, a trivia contest, and a bake sale. Volunteers were needed to help with organizing these activities, but the responsibilities seemed pretty straightforward and manageable.

Becca quickly sent a text to Sarah and Emma with the details. "We've got a new challenge ahead. It's not too big—just helping out with Spirit Week activities at school. It looks like it could be a fun way to get involved without too much pressure."

Sarah replied almost immediately. "That sounds perfect! It's a great way to contribute without overloading ourselves. Plus, we can all use a little fun amidst all the studying."

Emma's response was equally encouraging. "Absolutely. It's a chance to apply what we've learned and still be part of the school community. Count me in."

The girls made plans to meet the following day to discuss how they could contribute to Spirit Week. Becca felt a wave of relief as she realized that this new opportunity aligned perfectly with their current situation. It was a manageable way to stay engaged and make a positive impact without overwhelming themselves.

As Becca prepared for bed, she reflected on the day's events. Her thoughts were interrupted by a notification on her phone. It was a new email, but this time from the school's guidance office. The subject line read: "Important Update Regarding Graduation and Next Steps."

Her heart raced as she opened the email. The message detailed upcoming meetings for seniors to discuss graduation requirements and future plans. Becca was intrigued but also curious about what the next steps would entail.

The following morning, Becca met with Sarah and Emma at their usual spot in the library. They reviewed their plans for Spirit Week and brainstormed ideas for how they could each contribute. The conversation was light-hearted and full of laughter, but there was an underlying excitement about the new challenge ahead.

As they wrapped up their discussion, Becca glanced at her phone and noticed a message from Pastor John. The subject line read: "Re: Leadership Initiative and Your Role."

Becca's heart skipped a beat as she opened the message. Pastor John acknowledged their concerns and expressed understanding. He suggested they focus on the Spirit Week activities and participate in the leadership initiative as support roles rather than leaders, which would give them a chance to learn and grow without taking on too much at once.

Feeling reassured, Becca shared the update with Sarah and Emma. They were all relieved and excited about the prospect of being involved in a way that fit their current capabilities.

As the girls prepared for their next steps, Becca couldn't shake a lingering sense of anticipation. The final email she received about graduation and future plans hinted at new beginnings and challenges. With her friends by her side, Becca felt ready to face whatever came next.

Chapter 28

The day after their coffee shop meeting, Becca, Sarah, and Emma arrived at school, eager to start working on Spirit Week activities. The excitement of their new challenge was a welcome distraction from the usual routine of classes and assignments. As they walked through the halls, Becca couldn't help but feel a sense of anticipation about the new opportunities that lay ahead.

During their lunch break, the girls gathered in the library to finalize their plans. They divided the tasks among themselves: Becca would handle the themed dress-up day, Sarah would organize the trivia contest, and Emma would oversee the bake sale. Their discussion was filled with enthusiasm and laughter, and they felt confident in their abilities to manage the activities.

As the school day came to a close, Becca's phone buzzed with a new email notification. It was from the school's guidance office, following up on the previous email about graduation and future plans. The subject line read: "Important Update: Graduation Meeting Tomorrow."

Becca's heart skipped a beat as she opened the email. The message detailed an important meeting for all seniors to discuss graduation requirements, final exams, and plans for life after high school. Becca's mind raced with questions and concerns. Graduation was fast approaching, and the reality of what lay ahead was starting to sink in.

After school, Becca met up with Sarah and Emma. They shared their thoughts about the upcoming graduation meeting, each expressing a mix of excitement and wonder—Sarah's eyes lit up with anticipation, while Emma's voice carried a note of curiosity, and Becca found herself caught between both feelings.

"Can you believe we're almost done with high school?" Sarah asked, her voice tinged with disbelief. "It feels like just yesterday we were freshmen, trying to figure out where our classes were."

Emma nodded, a thoughtful expression on her face. "I know, right? It's exciting, but also a little scary. There's so much to think about—college applications, career choices, and everything else that comes with being an adult."

Becca listened to her friends, her own thoughts mirroring their sentiments. "Yeah, it's a lot to take in. "I'm excited about the future—the possibilities, new experiences, and opportunities waiting just around the corner fill me with anticipation. But at the same time, I'm also nervous about all the changes that come with it. The uncertainty, the fear of the unknown, and the thought of leaving behind what's familiar make my heart race. It's a mix of hope and hesitation, a feeling like I'm standing on the edge of something great, yet still unsure of my footing. I guess we just have to take it one step at a time."

Their conversation shifted to more immediate concerns, and they discussed their plans for Spirit Week. As they wrapped up their meeting, Becca felt a renewed sense of purpose. The support of her friends and the excitement of their shared activities gave her the confidence to face the challenges ahead.

That evening, Becca returned home to find her parents and Jason in the living room, discussing their plans for the weekend. Becca joined them, feeling a sense of comfort in the familiarity of their family routine. After dinner, she retreated to her room to check her email once more.

As she scrolled through her messages, one email stood out. It was from Pastor John, with the subject line: "Re: Leadership Initiative and

Your Role." Becca opened the email, her heart pounding with anticipation.

"Dear Becca,

I've spoken with the church leadership team about your concerns regarding the new leadership initiative. We understand that taking on a leadership role at this stage might be just a little too much, especially with your school responsibilities. We would love for you and your friends to participate as support roles rather than leaders. This way, you can gain experience and learn without the pressure of leading the initiative.

Thank you for your honesty and willingness to contribute. I'm confident that you will grow and thrive in this supportive environment.

Blessings, Pastor John"

Becca felt a wave of relief wash over her. The thought of participating in the initiative without the pressure of leading was a perfect compromise. She quickly sent a text to Sarah and Emma, sharing the update. They were all relieved and excited about the prospect of being involved in a way that suited their current capabilities.

The next day, Becca attended the graduation meeting with her classmates. The school counselor outlined the requirements for graduation, the schedule for final exams, and the steps needed to ensure a smooth transition to life after high school. Becca took careful notes, feeling a mix of excitement and uncertainty as the reality of graduation set in.

After the meeting, Becca met up with Sarah and Emma to discuss their plans for the future. They talked about their college applications, career aspirations, and the steps they needed to take to achieve their goals. The support and encouragement they offered each other were invaluable, and Becca felt grateful for their friendship.

As they walked to their next class, Becca received another email notification. This time, it was from the church, inviting her and her friends to participate in a special event to celebrate the end of Spirit

Week. The event would include a series of activities and a closing ceremony, where the participants would be recognized for their contributions.

Becca shared the news with Sarah and Emma, and they agreed to participate in the event. The anticipation of the upcoming activities and the support of her friends gave Becca a renewed sense of confidence.

That evening, as Becca settled into her room to study, she reflected on her journey so far. She thought about the challenges she had faced, the growth she had experienced, and the support she had received from her friends and family. She felt a deep sense of gratitude for the people in her life and the opportunities that had come her way.

However, just as she was about to close her laptop, another email notification popped up. This time, it was from the school's principal. The subject line read: "Urgent: Mandatory Meeting for All Seniors."

Becca's heart raced as she opened the email, her mind racing with possibilities. The message detailed a mandatory meeting for all seniors to discuss an important development that would impact their graduation plans. The meeting was scheduled for the next morning, and attendance was crucial.

Becca felt a surge of anxiety as she read the email. What could this new development be? The uncertainty of the situation left her feeling wary, but she knew she had to face it.

Chapter 29

The final senior meeting was a blend of excitement and nostalgia, filled with the buzz of students eagerly looking forward to their upcoming graduation. Principal Carter, a tall man with a welcoming presence, stood at the front of the auditorium, addressing the gathered crowd of students and teachers.

Thank you all for coming," Principal Carter began, his voice reflecting a genuine sense of gratitude. "As we approach the end of your high school journey, we have a special event planned: the Senior Showcase. This event will celebrate your achievements and give you a chance to reflect on your time here."

The room erupted with murmurs of curiosity and anticipation. Becca sat with Sarah and Emma, their faces a mix of excitement and curiosity. The Senior Showcase was more than just an opportunity to present—it was a chance to capture the essence of their high school experiences.

Principal Carter continued, "Each of you will have the opportunity to present a project or share an accomplishment that represents your journey. We want to celebrate not just your academic successes but also the growth and strength you've shown over the years.

Becca's heart raced as she processed the announcement. The idea of presenting something in front of their peers and teachers was both thrilling and intimidating. This was a chance to make their experiences meaningful, but the pressure was intense.

As the meeting concluded, Becca and her friends gathered near their lockers, discussing their plans. "So, what are you guys thinking?" Sarah asked, her eyes sparkling with excitement.

Emma shrugged. "It's a big opportunity. I'm thinking of focusing on the community service projects we've been involved in this year."

Becca nodded thoughtfully. "I was thinking we could highlight our personal growth—how we faced challenges, learned from them, and came out stronger. It's been a transformative year for us."

Sarah and Emma exchanged glances, nodding in agreement. "That sounds perfect," Emma said. "We've grown so much, and sharing that could be really powerful."

Just then, Mrs. Thompson approached with her usual warm smile. "I'm glad to see you all excited about the showcase. If you need any guidance or resources, I'm here to help. This is a great chance to show everyone what you've accomplished."

Becca smiled gratefully. "Thank you, Mrs. Thompson. We're definitely going to need some help with finalizing our presentation."

Later that evening, Becca sat at her desk, surrounded by notes and sketches for her presentation. The task felt challenging, but she was determined to make it meaningful. As she wrote, she reflected on the past year—the fears she had overcome, the friends she had made, and the lessons she had learned.

Her phone buzzed, breaking her concentration. It was a reminder from Sarah and Emma about their planning session scheduled for the next day, where they would finalize their ideas and practice their presentations. As she put her phone down, she felt a wave of anticipation and started mentally preparing for the busy day ahead.

The night before the showcase, Becca was caught between excitement and nervousness. Having come so far, this was her chance to share her journey with others. As she reviewed her notes, she reflected on the progress she'd made and felt a renewed sense of purpose and determination. The weight of the moment seemed to fuel her drive to make her presentation truly impactful.

On the day of the showcase, the school was abuzz with activity. Becca, Sarah, and Emma arrived early to make final adjustments. The atmosphere was electric, charged with anticipation and nervous energy. Becca took in the sight of her classmates and teachers, each immersed in their own preparations. The collective effort created a vibrant tapestry that highlighted the essence of their high school experience, making the day even more special.

As the time for the showcase approached, Becca's nerves began to return. Despite the confidence she had built up over the year, standing in front of a crowd still made her uneasy. She looked around the room, taking in the supportive faces of her friends and family. Pastor John was there too, offering a reassuring smile from the audience.

When the showcase finally began, Becca took a deep breath and stepped up to the stage. The lights were bright, and the audience's faces blurred into a sea of eager anticipation. As she looked out at the crowd, she saw familiar faces—friends, teachers, and mentors who had supported her throughout the year.

With a deep breath, Becca began her presentation. She spoke about the challenges she had faced, the growth she had experienced, and the importance of overcoming fears. Her voice, steady and clear, conveyed the journey she had taken. The audience listened intently, moved by her heartfelt words.

As she concluded her presentation, Becca felt a profound sense of accomplishment. The nervousness she had felt earlier was replaced by a sense of fulfillment. She had shared her story, and it had left a meaningful impact on those who were there to support her.

The event proceeded smoothly, and the feedback from her peers and teachers was overwhelmingly positive. As Becca left the stage, she felt a mix of relief and satisfaction. This was the culmination of her journey, a celebration of her growth.

As the showcase came to an end, Becca and her friends gathered to reflect on the event. They were exhausted but exhilarated, their faces glowing with the afterglow of their hard work. They shared stories of their experiences, each recounting the moments that stood out and the challenges they had overcome. The sense of achievement was evident as they marveled at how far they had come. This was more than just a showcase; it was a testament to their dedication and growth, a milestone they would remember with a deep sense of fulfillment.

But just as they were beginning to relax, Becca received a message on her phone. It was from the school, announcing an upcoming event that would require their participation. The message hinted at something significant, leaving Becca and her friends curious to find out what it was.

As Becca read the message, she couldn't help but wonder what new challenge awaited them. The year had been full of surprises, and it seemed like there was one more to come.

Chapter 30

The morning of the upcoming challenge arrived with a mix of anticipation and nerves. The email from the school had revealed an exciting yet demanding task: the opportunity for seniors to organize and execute a final community event before graduation. The event was designed to showcase their skills, leadership, and creativity—traits they had developed over their high school years.

Becca, Sarah, and Emma met at their favorite coffee shop to discuss the new challenge. They had already accomplished a lot this year, but this new task was different. It required them to take charge and work collaboratively to create an event that would leave a lasting impression on their community.

"I still can't believe we're going to be organizing this event ourselves," Emma said, stirring her coffee absentmindedly. "It sounds like a huge responsibility, but it's also a great chance for us to show what we've learned."

Sarah nodded in agreement. "It definitely feels like a big step up from the showcase. Still, we've managed to pull off some pretty amazing things together this year."

Becca took a deep breath, her mind racing with thoughts of what needed to be done. "We need to plan everything—from the theme to the logistics. And we have to make sure it reflects everything we've learned and the impact we want to have."

Emma looked at her thoughtfully. "It's a lot of work, but we've tackled challenges before. And if we manage it well, it could be a great way to end our senior year."

Becca agreed, but she felt a tinge of anxiety. "I'm just worried about the scale of it all. We've never done anything this big. What if we miss something important or it doesn't turn out the way we hope?"

Sarah reached across the table and placed a reassuring hand on Becca's. "We'll tackle this one step at a time. With the backing of Pastor John and our families, we're more than capable of making it happen."

The three friends spent the next few hours brainstorming ideas and outlining their plans. They divided tasks among themselves, focusing on areas where they felt they could make the most impact. Becca would take charge of the event's overall theme and coordination, Sarah would handle logistics and outreach, and Emma would manage the creative aspects and design.

By the end of their meeting, they had a clear plan and a sense of purpose. The challenge was daunting, but it also felt invigorating. They were ready to put their skills to the test and create something meaningful for their community.

The morning of the big day arrived with a noticeable buzz of excitement and a tinge of nerves. The final community event, organized by Becca, Sarah, and Emma, was set to be the highlight of their senior year. It was an opportunity for the students to showcase their skills and give back to the community that had supported them throughout their high school journey.

The event was held at the local community center, which had been transformed into a vibrant hub of activity. The theme was "Celebrating Community," and the trio had planned a day filled with interactive booths, performances, and activities designed to engage and entertain attendees of all ages.

Becca arrived early, her heart racing as she surveyed the scene. The center was alive with the hum of preparation. Tables were being set up for the various booths, and colorful decorations brightened every corner, reflecting the theme of the event. Volunteers and fellow students, who had eagerly signed up to help, were busy setting up displays and arranging seating.

Becca took a moment to appreciate the effort that had gone into organizing the event. Her role had been to oversee the overall theme and coordination. She had worked tirelessly to ensure that every detail was perfect, from the layout of the booths to the schedule of activities.

Sarah was busy at the logistics desk, checking in volunteers and coordinating last-minute details. She had taken charge of ensuring that everything ran smoothly, from managing the schedule to handling any unforeseen issues.

Emma, on the other hand, was in her element, overseeing the creative aspects of the event. She had designed the promotional materials, including posters and flyers, and had set up a photo booth where attendees could take pictures to remember the day. Emma's artistic touch was evident in every corner of the venue, adding a personal and vibrant touch to the event.

As the guests began to arrive, Becca felt a mix of excitement and nerves. She greeted visitors with a warm smile, making sure they were welcomed and informed about the various activities. The event featured a range of attractions, including a talent showcase where local performers took the stage, interactive booths where participants could engage in hands-on activities, and a raffle with prizes donated by local businesses.

The highlight of the day was a community mural project, where people of all ages could contribute to a large mural that represented the spirit of the community. Becca, Sarah, and Emma had worked with local artists to design the mural, and it quickly became a focal point of the event. Guests gathered around, adding their own artistic touches and leaving behind messages of hope and unity.

Throughout the day, Becca moved through the crowd, checking in with her friends and ensuring everything was running smoothly. There were moments of joy as she saw everyone enjoying the event, and moments of stress as she handled unexpected issues. A small technical glitch with the sound system had caused a brief delay, but with quick thinking and teamwork, the issue was resolved, and the event continued seamlessly.

As the event drew to a close, Becca felt a deep sense of satisfaction. The positive feedback from those who attended, the smiles on their faces, and the sense of community that had been fostered made all the hard work worth it. The day had been a testament to their growth and the strength of their friendships.

Just as they were starting to clean up, Becca's phone buzzed with a new message. It was from Pastor John, and the subject line read: "A New Opportunity."

Becca's heart skipped a beat as she opened the message. It briefly mentioned a potential new project that would require her skills and creativity, and it suggested a meeting to discuss it further. The message ended with an invitation to discuss the details at a time convenient for her.

Becca shared the message with Sarah and Emma, her curiosity and excitement evident. "Looks like there might be another opportunity coming our way," she said, her eyes sparkling with anticipation.

Sarah and Emma exchanged excited glances. "Whatever it is, I'm sure it'll be another great experience," Emma said.

As they wrapped up their work and prepared to head home, Becca couldn't help but feel a renewed sense of purpose. The event had been a success, and the day had been a testament to her growth and the strength of her friendships. With the new opportunity on the horizon, Becca felt ready to embrace whatever came next.

Chapter 31

The following morning, Becca woke with a mix of excitement and nervousness. The event had gone well, and her presentation was well-received. She felt a deep sense of satisfaction, but the new email from Pastor John added another layer of anticipation.

After breakfast, Becca met Sarah and Emma at the local park for a leisurely stroll and to share their thoughts on the event. The park was a tranquil spot, with lush greenery and the sound of birds chirping providing a soothing backdrop for their conversation.

"I can't believe it's finally over," Sarah said, stirring her coffee. "You did an amazing job, Becca. I feel like we really made an impact."

Emma nodded in agreement. "Definitely. But I keep thinking about what Pastor John mentioned. What do you think it could be?"

Becca took a deep breath, trying to calm her nerves. "I'm not sure. The email was pretty vague. But whatever it is, I'm willing to give it a shot."

The conversation shifted to their plans for the summer and beyond. They discussed their upcoming finals and graduation preparations, but Becca couldn't shake the feeling that something significant was on the horizon.

Later that day, Becca received a call from Pastor John. "Hi Becca, I wanted to talk to you about that email I sent. There's an opportunity for you to get involved with a new community outreach project."

Becca's heart raced. "What kind of project?"

"It's a bit different from what you've done before," Pastor John explained. "The project involves organizing a series of workshops aimed at helping people in the community with practical skills, like budgeting and career planning. You won't be leading it; instead, you'll help coordinate the sessions and support the team."

Becca felt a wave of relief mixed with anxiety. "That sounds interesting. I'm not sure I'm ready to lead something like this, though."

Pastor John's voice was reassuring. "You don't need to lead. Your role will be to assist with planning and organizing, ensuring everything runs smoothly. You'll have support from experienced team members, and I believe it's a great way for you to continue growing."

After the call, Becca felt both eager and uncertain. She discussed the opportunity with her family that evening, sharing her mixed feelings about the new challenge.

Her mom smiled encouragingly. "This sounds like a wonderful chance for you to continue making a positive impact. I believe you're ready for this," she said with encouragement. "You've shown so much progress and strength over the past year. This new challenge is just another opportunity for you to put all that growth into action."

Her dad added, "If you're unsure, take it one step at a time. You don't have to have everything figured out right now."

As she prepared for bed, Becca reflected on the new opportunity. She envisioned herself working behind the scenes, coordinating with team members, and managing logistics. The idea of organizing without leading directly felt like a manageable step forward.

The next morning, as Becca walked into school, the excitement of the upcoming new project mingled with her ongoing preparations for finals and graduation. She felt supported by her friends, family, and community.

In the days that followed, Becca attended initial meetings with Pastor John and the team. She was introduced to her role as the coordinator, responsible for scheduling, communicating with speakers, and ensuring the workshops ran smoothly. She worked closely with others who had more experience, learning from them and contributing her organizational skills.

During a planning meeting, Becca took notes as the team discussed various aspects of the workshops. She helped create a schedule, arranged for resources, and coordinated with volunteers. While she wasn't in charge, her contributions were vital to the project's success.

As Becca glanced at her phone one afternoon, she saw a new message from Pastor John: "We'll meet next week to discuss the final details of the workshops. Looking forward to working with you."

Becca's heart fluttered with excitement. The journey ahead promised to be both challenging and rewarding. She felt ready to embrace the opportunity and support the project in every way she could.

With a sense of purpose and support, Becca prepared for the new role. She knew she was stepping into a new chapter, one that would help her grow and make a meaningful contribution to her community. The event day approached, and Becca was ready to face the challenges and opportunities it would bring.

Chapter 32

Becca woke up early on Saturday, her anticipation building for the community outreach event she had been preparing for. The sun was just starting to cast its first light through her window, and she could feel the buzz of excitement running through her veins. She had spent the last few days meticulously organizing every detail, but today would be the real test of her efforts.

After a quick breakfast, she headed out, feeling a mix of nervousness and eagerness. When she arrived at the community center, the bustling activity was already in full swing. Volunteers were everywhere—setting up tables, arranging chairs, and preparing materials. The center was alive with energy, and Becca couldn't help but smile at the sight.

Emma and Sarah were among the early arrivals, already hard at work. Emma was organizing the resources and checking off the list of supplies, while Sarah managed the schedule for the day. Their enthusiasm was infectious, and Becca joined them, diving into the tasks with a sense of purpose.

"Morning, Becca!" Emma greeted, her voice full of cheer. "We're almost ready to go. Just a heads-up, though—the guest speaker is running a bit behind."

Becca nodded, understanding the situation. She began helping with the registration table, setting up name tags, and making sure all the materials were neatly arranged. As she worked, she noticed the growing concern among some of the volunteers. The delay with the guest speaker was starting to create a ripple of unease.

While Becca was organizing the materials, Sarah approached her with a worried look. "We've hit a snag with the tech setup for the presentations," she said. "Can you help us sort it out?"

Becca quickly assessed the situation and realized that the projector wasn't connecting properly with the laptop. It was a tech issue that required immediate attention. Working alongside Sarah, Becca managed to troubleshoot the problem, adjusting cables and configuring settings until everything was back on track. The guest speaker's delay was a minor setback, but with the tech problem resolved, they could proceed smoothly.

As the event unfolded, the atmosphere was lively and positive despite the earlier hiccups. Becca was impressed by the turnout and the engagement of everyone. Her parents, who had volunteered to help with the cleanup, arrived later in the day. She spotted them amidst the crowd and felt a wave of relief and gratitude.

"Hey, Mom, Dad," Becca greeted as she walked over to them. "Thanks so much for coming and helping out."

Her mother smiled warmly, her eyes filled with admiration. "It's incredible to see you organizing something like this, Becca."

Her father, carrying a box of leftover materials, added, "It's wonderful to see you taking charge and making a difference. Your hard work and dedication are truly impressive."

Their words of encouragement meant a lot to Becca. She felt a deep sense of accomplishment as she worked alongside her family to clean up the community center. The afternoon was filled with laughter as volunteers and family members pitched in to put everything back in order.

Becca, Emma, and Sarah tackled the final tasks together, their teamwork ensuring that the center was spotless by the end of the day. They exchanged stories and shared their highlights from the event, their bond growing stronger with each moment. The cleanup was a team effort, with everyone contributing to a successful wrap-up of the outreach.

As the sun began to set, Becca took a moment to reflect on the day. The event had been a success, despite the initial challenges. She felt a profound sense of satisfaction, knowing that their hard work had made a difference in the community. The positive feedback from everyone and the smooth resolution of the tech issues were testaments to their dedication.

By the time Becca arrived home, she was exhausted but content. She had managed to balance the excitement of the event with the practical aspects of managing a busy day. The experience had been both rewarding and demanding, and she was ready to embrace the next challenge.

On Monday morning, Becca walked into school with a renewed sense of purpose. The familiar buzz of the hallways was a notable shift from the quiet of the community center, but she felt ready to tackle whatever came her way. Finals were approaching, and the pressure was building. The weekend's activities had been a refreshing change, but now it was time to focus on her academic responsibilities.

Becca couldn't help but reflect on how far she had come. The outreach event had been a milestone, a tangible result of her growth and dedication. As she navigated the school corridors, she felt a sense of readiness for the upcoming challenges. The positive experiences from the event had given her the confidence to face her finals and other responsibilities with a fresh perspective.

The day unfolded with its usual pace, and Becca found herself juggling between her classes and the growing list of things to do. Her mind was still partially wrapped around the community event, but she knew she needed to shift her focus back to her studies. She hoped that the skills and experiences from the outreach would help her approach her exams with renewed determination and clarity.

As the final bell rang and the school day came to an end, Becca felt a mix of anticipation and relief. The weekend had been a whirlwind of activity, but it had also reaffirmed her belief in her abilities and the support of her friends and family. She was prepared to face the upcoming challenges, whatever they might be, with optimism and determination.

Little did she know that the coming days would bring new opportunities and challenges, each one shaping her journey in unexpected ways. The sense of accomplishment from the outreach event was just the beginning of a new chapter in her life, and Becca was prepared to face it head-on.

Chapter 33

Monday passed in a blur as Becca navigated through her classes with a renewed sense of purpose. Her thoughts frequently drifted back to the community outreach event, but the approaching finals demanded her full attention. The blend of academic pressure and lingering excitement from the weekend created a unique atmosphere of anticipation.

By the time she got home, Becca felt the weight of the day. She sank into her desk chair, opened her laptop, and reviewed her notes. As she studied, her phone buzzed with messages of encouragement from Emma and Sarah. They had all decided to meet up later in the week to discuss their plans for the upcoming summer. The support and connection with her friends continued to be a cornerstone of Becca's journey.

The week unfolded with a mix of study sessions and moments of reflection. Becca found herself frequently revisiting the weekend's events in her mind. The success of the outreach had bolstered her confidence, but she was acutely aware that the road ahead was still filled with challenges. Finals were fast approaching, and the pressure was intense.

On Wednesday, Becca received an email from the school administration congratulating her on being nominated for the school's "Most Improved Student" award. The nomination was based on her academic achievements and her contributions to the community. Becca felt a surge of emotions—surprise, gratitude, and a touch of disbelief.

She had come a long way from the timid girl who was afraid of her own shadow.

"Wow, Becca! This is amazing!" Sarah exclaimed when Becca shared the news during lunch.

Emma nodded in agreement. "You've worked so hard, and it's really paying off. We are so happy for you!"

Their words filled Becca with warmth. She realized that this nomination was more than just recognition; it was a reflection of her progress and the support she had received from those around her.

The days flew by as Becca and her friends focused on their studies. The end of the school year was fast approaching, and with it, the promise of graduation and new beginnings. Becca balanced her time between preparing for exams and reflecting on her achievements. The sense of accomplishment she felt was balanced by a clear recognition of the effort required to complete the journey ahead.

The much-anticipated day of the awards ceremony had arrived. Becca dressed carefully, choosing a simple yet elegant outfit. Her parents, who had been her unwavering support system, accompanied her to the event. The school auditorium was filled with students, teachers, and families, all gathered to celebrate the year's accomplishments.

As Becca walked onto the stage to accept her award, she scanned the audience and spotted Pastor John sitting among the attendees. His presence was a reassuring reminder of the journey she had undertaken. When the principal handed her the award, Becca felt a swell of emotion. This moment was a culmination of her efforts, a tangible acknowledgment of her growth and resilience.

The applause that followed was deeply moving. Becca took a deep breath and smiled, feeling a profound sense of fulfillment. She glanced at her parents, whose faces were beaming. Her friends cheered loudly, their support unwavering.

After the ceremony, Becca's family and friends gathered around her, offering congratulations and words of encouragement. Pastor John approached, his eyes reflecting his genuine admiration for her achievements.

"Becca, you've made incredible progress. This is only the beginning," he said warmly. "I look forward to seeing where your path leads you next."

Becca nodded, feeling a surge of determination. "Thank you, Pastor John. I couldn't have done it without everyone." She took a moment to appreciate the support she had received, knowing that it had made all the difference.

The evening was filled with celebration and reflection. Becca's thoughts were a whirlwind of emotions as she considered the milestones she had achieved and the challenges she had overcome. The journey had been difficult, but each step highlighted her determination and the steadfast support of her community.

As the night drew to a close, Becca found herself alone in her room, reflecting on the day's events. The award was a significant milestone, but it also marked a turning point. She knew that the path ahead was still unfolding. There were fears to face and challenges to overcome. But for the first time, Becca felt a deep sense of confidence in her ability to navigate whatever lay ahead.

The next Monday, Becca was back in school, preparing for her final exams. The pressure was intense, but she approached it with a newfound sense of calm. The recognition she had received bolstered her confidence, reminding her of the progress she had made.

During a break between classes, Becca met up with Emma and Sarah in the library. They discussed their study plans and shared tips for the upcoming exams. The support and encouragement they offered each other were invaluable.

"We're ready," Sarah said confidently. "We've put in the effort, and we're prepared for whatever challenges come next." Emma nodded in agreement. "Let's finish strong and make this a year to remember."

Becca smiled, feeling a surge of motivation. She was ready to tackle the finals and face the future with confidence. The experience had been tough, but it had also been incredibly rewarding.

As the days passed, Becca focused on her studies, drawing strength from the support of her friends and family. With graduation just around the corner, there was an added sense of enthusiasm in the air. She knew that the end of the school year was just the beginning of a new chapter in her life.

On the Friday before finals week, Becca received another email. This one was from the community center, inviting her to participate in a new mentorship program for younger students during the summer. The program was designed to help students develop their skills and confidence, much like Becca had over the past year.

Becca's emotions were a mix of eagerness and uncertainty as she read the email. This was a new opportunity to give back and support others on their journeys. It was also a chance to continue her own growth and development.

She shared the news with her parents over dinner that evening. "I think this could be a great opportunity," she said. "But it's also a bit intimidating. I've never done anything like this before."

Her father smiled encouragingly. "Becca, you've already done so much. This is just another important step. You'll do great."

Her mother nodded in agreement. "And we'll be here to support you every step of the way."

Becca felt a sense of reassurance. She knew that she wasn't alone on this journey. With the support of her family and friends, she was ready to embrace this new opportunity.

As the weekend approached, Becca prepared for the upcoming finals with a sense of determination. The community outreach event had been a milestone, but the journey was far from over. There were still challenges to face and goals to achieve.

Monday morning arrived, Becca walked into school with a sense of purpose. The final exams were the last hurdle before graduation, and she was ready to give it her all she had. The recognition she had received and the support of her loved ones had strengthened her resolve.

The week of finals was intense, but Becca approached each exam with confidence. She drew on the skills and resilience she had developed over the past year, knowing that she was capable of overcoming any challenge.

By the time Friday arrived, Becca felt a mix of exhaustion and relief. The exams were over, and the excitement of graduation was intense. She spent the weekend thinking aboutt her experiences, feeling deeply grateful for the people and the moments that had influenced her.

As Becca stood on the stage during the graduation ceremony, surrounded by her classmates, she felt a deep sense of accomplishment. The journey had been challenging, but it had also been incredibly rewarding. She had grown in ways she never imagined possible, a true reflection of her progress and the support she received along the way.

Looking out at the audience, Becca saw her parents, Pastor John, and her friends, all beaming with pride and support. She knew that this was just the beginning of a new chapter in her life. There were still challenges to face and goals to achieve, but she was ready to embrace the future with confidence and faith.

The ceremony concluded with cheers and applause, marking the end of one chapter and the beginning of another. Becca felt a sense of excitement and anticipation for what lay ahead. She was ready to continue growing and achieving her dreams.

As the evening drew to a close, Becca gathered with her family and friends to celebrate. They shared stories, laughter, and words of encouragement. The support and love she felt were a clear sign of the strength of her relationships and the impact of her experiences.

In the midst of the celebration, Becca spotted her younger brother, Jason, making his way through the crowd. His eyes lit up when he saw her.

"Becca!" he called out, running up to her with a big grin. "You did amazing up there! It's wonderful to see all your hard work paying off."

Becca hugged him tightly. "Thanks, Jason. It means a lot to hear that from you. I couldn't have done it without all the support from you and Mom and Dad."

Jason looked around, his excitement evident. "It's so cool seeing everyone here. I can't wait for my own graduation in two years. Hopefully, I'll have as many great experiences as you did."

Becca ruffled his hair, smiling at his enthusiasm. "You will. Just make sure you keep pushing yourself and stay true to who you are. It's going to be an amazing journey for you."

As they chatted, Becca's parents joined them, bringing refreshments and joining in the celebration. They talked about their plans for the summer and the upcoming changes. The warmth and love of the moment were a fitting end to a significant chapter in Becca's life.

In the quiet moments that followed, Becca took a deep breath and reflected on the journey so far. The accomplishments she had achieved were significant, but they were just the beginning. The future was full of possibilities, and she was ready to embrace it with open arms.

The following Sunday, the church held a special recognition for the graduates during the service. Each graduate received a small gift and a prayer from Pastor John, who spoke words of encouragement and faith over them. As Becca stood with the other graduates, she felt a sense of community and belonging that warmed her heart.

As the service ended, Becca's thoughts turned to the future. She had accomplished a major goal, but there were still many new experiences awaiting her. With her exams completed and graduation behind her, she was prepared to face the next chapter with the same determination and faith that had guided her throughout high school.

As she left the church and headed home, Becca felt a sense of calm and readiness for whatever lay ahead.

Chapter 34

As Becca walked home from church, the warmth of the afternoon sun on her face, she couldn't help but reflect on the whirlwind of events that had led her to this point. Graduation had been a significant milestone, a day brimming with emotions, memories, and a sense of accomplishment that was still settling in. The church's recognition ceremony had been a touching reminder of the support she'd received alonga the way. Yet, beneath the surface, she felt a stirring, an awareness that something more was coming—a final test that would either solidify her transformation or challenge it in ways she hadn't anticipated.

The following week, life began to settle into a new rhythm. With graduation behind her, Becca started thinking about the future. College was on the horizon, and though the idea was exciting, it also brought a wave of uncertainty. What would it be like to leave home, to navigate a new environment, to face challenges she couldn't yet foresee? These questions swirled in her mind as she prepared for the next chapter of her life.

One afternoon, as she sat in her room sorting through college paperwork, Becca received a phone call that would set the stage for her final test. It was Pastor John, his voice as steady and reassuring as ever.

"Becca, I know you've been through a lot these past few months, and I've seen how much you've grown," he began. "There's something I'd like to discuss with you—an opportunity that I believe could be a turning point for you."

Becca listened intently as Pastor John explained the situation. The church had recently begun working with a local youth shelter, offering support to teens who had nowhere else to go. The shelter was looking for volunteers to help organize and run a series of workshops designed to equip these young people with essential life skills. It was a difficult task, one that needed kindness, patience, and a real understanding of what it means to face fears and conquer them.

"I'd like you to be involved," Pastor John said. "I think you have a unique perspective that could really connect with these kids. You wouldn't be leading on your own—there will be a team of us working together—but your voice could be incredibly powerful."

Becca's heart raced as she thought about the magnitude of what was being asked of her. This was far beyond anything she had done before, and it would force her to face some of her biggest fears. Could she really do this? Was she ready to take on such a responsibility?

"I believe in you, Becca," Pastor John continued. "You've shown incredible strength, and I know you can handle this. But it's entirely up to you. Take some time to think about it, and let me know what you decide."

After they hung up, Becca sat in silence, her mind a whirlwind of thoughts. This was the test she had sensed was coming—the moment that would require her to draw on everything she had learned, to step out in faith and trust that she was capable of more than she ever imagined.

That evening, as she knelt by her bed in prayer, Becca sought guidance. She poured out her fears, her doubts, and her hopes, asking for the strength to make the right decision. In the quiet that followed, she felt a deep sense of peace wash over her, a calm assurance that she was not alone.

The next day, she met with Sarah and Emma at their favorite coffee shop. They had become her closest friends, a source of unwavering support, and she knew she could trust them with her concerns.

After sharing what Pastor John had proposed, Becca looked at her friends expectantly. "What do you think? Am I really ready for something like this?"

Sarah leaned forward, her eyes filled with confidence. "Yes, Becca, I believe you can do this. You've come so far, and this is a great chance to help others who are going through the same struggles you faced. We'll support you all the way."

Emma nodded in agreement. "You've got so much to offer, Becca. Even though it might seem challenging at the moment, but sometimes that's what turns out to be the most rewarding."

Encouraged by their words, Becca began to see the possibility that maybe, just maybe, she was ready for this challenge. Later that evening, Becca sent a message to Pastor John. "I've talked with Sarah and Emma, and I'm ready to take on the role. I'll give it my best."

As the day of the first workshop approached, familiar feelings of anxiety began to creep in. What if she messed up? What if she couldn't connect with the kids? The doubts were relentless, but this time, she knew how to face them.

Standing in front of the mirror on the big day, Becca took a deep breath. She reminded herself of all she had overcome—every fear faced, every victory won. She wasn't the same person she had been at the start of this journey. Though the road ahead was uncertain, she was ready to take the next step.

As she arrived at the church, she was greeted by Pastor John and the rest of the team. The atmosphere was buzzing with anticipation, and Becca felt a mixture of nerves and excitement. The workshop began, and as she started speaking to the group of teens, something remarkable happened. The fears that had been gnawing at her started to fade, replaced by a sense of purpose and conviction.

Throughout the day, there were moments of doubt and moments of triumph. Becca found herself connecting with the teens in ways she hadn't expected, sharing her story and listening to theirs. By the end of the workshop, she felt an overwhelming sense of fulfillment—a realization that this was exactly where she was meant to be.

But as the day drew to a close, Pastor John pulled her aside, his expression serious.

"Becca, there's something else I need to tell you," he said, his tone grave. "We've just received news that one of the teens in our group is facing a critical situation—something that could have a major impact on her future. She's going to need all the support that she can get, and I believe you're the right person to help guide her through this."

The weight of his words settled on Becca's shoulders as she realized that the final test of her transformation was still to come.

Chapter 35

The gravity of Pastor John's words lingered in Becca's mind as she left the church that day. She knew this was the moment that would test everything she had learned, every bit of courage she had fought to gain. The summer sun was beginning to dip below the horizon, casting long shadows on the quiet streets as she walked home. It was a peaceful evening, but Becca's thoughts were anything but calm.

That night, sleep was hard to come by. She tossed and turned in bed, her mind racing with thoughts of the teen Pastor John had mentioned—Maria. What kind of critical situation was she facing? How could Becca, who had just begun to navigate her own challenges, possibly be the one to guide her? Despite the anxiety, there was also a sense of purpose—a calling she couldn't ignore. She had come so far, and now it was time to put everything into practice.

The next morning, Becca made her way to the church early, wanting to prepare herself mentally and spiritually for what lay ahead. The church was quiet, the usual hustle and bustle absent in the early hours. She found a secluded corner in the sanctuary and sat down, closing her eyes and letting the silence envelop her. With a deep breath, she began to pray, seeking clarity and strength.

"Lord, I'm scared," she whispered, her voice trembling slightly. "But I trust that You have brought me here for a reason. Help me to be the support Maria needs, and give me the wisdom to know how to help her."

As she prayed, a deep sense of peace washed over her, quieting her fears. It wasn't that the situation had changed, but rather that she felt assured she wasn't facing it alone. With renewed resolve, Becca rose from her seat, ready to take on the challenge ahead.

Later that day, Becca met Maria for the first time. She was a quiet girl, with long dark hair that fell over her eyes as if she were trying to hide from the world. The moment their eyes met, Becca felt a connection, a shared understanding of what it meant to face fear and uncertainty. Maria was reserved, speaking in short sentences and avoiding eye contact, but Becca could sense the depth of her struggles.

Their initial conversations were slow and cautious. Maria didn't trust easily, and Becca understood that. She didn't push, didn't pry. Instead, she offered Maria a safe space to talk when she was ready. They spent time together at the church, sometimes in silence, sometimes sharing small pieces of their lives. Becca found herself thinking back to her own journey, how difficult it had been to open up, to trust, to believe that someone else could understand.

As the days turned into weeks, Maria began to open up more. She shared bits of her story—how she had been abandoned by her parents, how she had bounced from one foster home to another, never feeling like she truly belonged anywhere. Becca listened closely, feeling a deep sadness for the girl who had endured so much at such a young age.

"You remind me of myself," Becca said one afternoon as they sat together in the church garden. The air was warm, the scent of blooming flowers filling the space around them. "I used to be so afraid of everything—of people, of failing, of not being good enough. But I learned that those fears don't have to control us. We can take small steps, little by little, to overcome them."

Maria looked at Becca with wide eyes, as if seeing her in a new light. "How did you do it?" she asked quietly. "How did you stop being afraid?"

Becca smiled softly, thinking about all the key moments that had made a difference in her life. "It wasn't easy, and I didn't do it alone. I had people who supported me, who believed in me even when I couldn't believe in myself. And I learned to trust in God's plan, even when I didn't understand it. It's still a work in progress, but I'm not as scared as I used to be."

Maria nodded, her expression thoughtful. "I want to be brave like you," she murmured.

"You already are," Becca replied gently. "You've survived so much, and you're still here, still fighting. That takes courage."

As the days passed, Becca continued to meet with Maria, offering not just advice but also a listening ear and a caring heart. She watched as Maria slowly began to gain confidence, to believe that she could have a future that was different from her past. It was a slow process, with setbacks along the way, but Becca was patient. She knew that healing and growth took time.

During this period, Becca's own life was also shifting. With graduation and high school behind her, she had reached a major turning point, marking the beginning of a new chapter. She had started preparing for college, filling out forms, making lists of what she would need, and mentally preparing herself for the big change. The thought of leaving home was both exciting and unsettling. What would it be like to live on her own, to be responsible for herself in a new place?

It was during this time that Becca met Sean. They crossed paths at a community event where both were volunteering. Sean was kind, thoughtful, and had a gentle strength that Becca found comforting. He was a few years older, already in college, and had a way of making her feel at ease whenever they talked. They quickly became friends, their shared experiences in helping others, creating a bond between the two of them.

Sean had his own story, one filled with challenges and growth, and as they spent more time together, Becca found herself opening up to him in ways she hadn't with anyone else. There was something about Sean that made her feel understood, as if he could see beyond the surface to the person she was becoming.

One evening, after they had spent the day volunteering together, they sat on a bench overlooking the river, watching the sunset. The sky was painted in shades of orange and pink, the water reflecting the colors like a mirror.

"Do you ever get scared?" Becca asked, breaking the comfortable silence between them.

Sean glanced at her, his expression thoughtful. "All the time," he admitted. "But I've learned that it's okay to be scared. It's how we deal with that fear that matters. I think you've shown incredible strength in how you've faced your fears."

Becca felt a warmth spread through her chest at his words. "I've had a lot of help," she said with a small smile. "And I've learned that it's okay to lean on others when I need to."

Sean nodded, his gaze returning to the horizon. "I'm glad you feel that way. It's important to have people in your life who you can trust, who can help you see things from a different perspective."

Their friendship deepened, and Becca began to realize that her journey wasn't just about overcoming fear—it was also about finding connections, understanding, and love in unexpected places. With Sean, she found someone who understood her struggles, who supported her, and who was willing to walk alongside her.

As the summer wore on, Becca continued to help Maria, building a relationship that was rooted in trust and mutual respect. And as she did, she found herself reflecting on her own life that had brought her to this point. From the timid girl who was afraid of her own shadow to a young woman who was helping others find their way, Becca had undergone a transformation that was nothing short of miraculous.

The final test had come, and Becca had faced it head-on, relying on her faith, her friends, and the lessons she had learned along the way. Now, as she looked toward the future, she felt a sense of calm and confidence that she had never known before.

But as she stood on the brink of this new beginning, Becca knew that her journey was far from over. There would be new challenges, new fears to face, and new opportunities to grow. And as she took Sean's hand, feeling the warmth of his presence beside her, she knew that whatever lay ahead, she was ready.

Epilogue

A few years had passed since Becca's life had taken that transformative turn. She now stood in the kitchen of her cozy home, the morning sun streaming through the windows as she prepared breakfast. The aroma of coffee filled the air, and the soft sounds of birds chirping outside added to the serene atmosphere.

Becca glanced at the framed wedding photo on the counter. It had been a beautiful day, filled with love and joy as she and Sean exchanged vows. Their journey together had been a testament to the power of faith, love, and the courage to face life's challenges head-on. Sean had been her rock, her confidant, and her greatest supporter, and now they were embarking on a new chapter together.

As she absentmindedly placed a hand on her growing belly, Becca felt a wave of emotion wash over her. She was expecting their first child, a blessing that filled her with both excitement and a hint of nervousness. The thought of becoming a mother was thrilling, yet at the same time a little unsettling, but Becca knew that she was ready for this new role. She had prepared her for it in ways she never could have imagined.

The years had been kind to Becca, but they had also been filled with challenges. She had faced each one with the strength and resilience that had come to define her. The young woman who had once lived in the shadow of fear had blossomed into someone who embraced life with open arms. Her faith had deepened, and she had learned to trust in the path that lay before her, even when it was uncertain.

Becca's transformation had not gone unnoticed. She had become a source of inspiration for others, sharing her story at various events and helping those who were struggling with their own fears. The work she had done with the youth at the church had grown into a larger outreach program, one that continued to touch the lives of many young people. It was a labor of love, one that brought her immense fulfillment.

As she stood in the kitchen, lost in thought, Sean entered the room. He wrapped his arms around her from behind, resting his chin on her shoulder. "Good morning," he said, his voice warm and affectionate. "How are you feeling?"

"Better now that you're here," Becca replied, leaning back into him. She felt a sense of peace in his embrace, a reminder that they were in this together.

They stood like that for a moment, savoring the quiet of the morning before the day began. Becca knew that life would continue to bring challenges, but she also knew that she had the strength to face them. She had learned that fear did not have to control her life and that faith, love, and determination were powerful tools for overcoming any obstacle that came her way.

As they sat down to breakfast, Sean took her hand in his. "We've come a long way, haven't we?" he said, his eyes filled with love and admiration.

"We have," Becca agreed, smiling at him. "And I wouldn't change a thing."

She looked out the window, her mind drifting to the future. She knew that there were still many adventures to come, many lessons to learn, and many opportunities to allow her to grow. But she also knew that she was no longer the same person who had once been paralyzed by fear. She had found her courage, her faith, and her purpose.

As she thought about the child growing inside of her, Becca felt a surge of hope and excitement. She was ready to pass on the lessons she had learned, to nurture and guide this new life with the same love and support that had been given to her. She knew that she and Sean would create a home filled with love, faith, and have the courage to face whatever challenges might come their way.

And as she looked back, Becca felt a deep sense of gratitude. The path had not always been easy, but it had been worth every struggle, every tear, and every victory. Her life was a powerful example of transformation, and she hoped her story would inspire others to find the courage to face their own fears.

In the end, Becca realized that life wasn't about avoiding fear but about embracing it, learning from it, and growing stronger because of it. Her hope was that others would understand that, no matter how challenging the journey might seem, with faith, love, and courage, anything is possible.

Acknowledgments

I would like to express my gratitude to Carol Taylor for her enduring support and guidance regarding cover and title decisions.

I also want to extend my thanks to Estella Ward for her assistance with both the cover and title decisions, as well as her support with the picture choices.

Don't miss out!

Visit the website below and you can sign up to receive emails whenever Cris Hoxie publishes a new book. There's no charge and no obligation.

https://books2read.com/r/B-A-PJFBB-IRPWE

BOOKS2READ

Connecting independent readers to independent writers.

Also by Cris Hoxie

Chronicles Of Hope
Quest For Courage

Standalone
Embracing the Armor of God

Watch for more at https://authorcrishoxie.wixsite.com/
authorcrishoxie.

About the Author

Cris Hoxie has spent most of her life in northern Michigan, where her passion for reading blossomed into a career as a book reviewer and devotional writer for a Facebook community. Growing up surrounded by the beauty of northern Michigan, Cris developed a lasting love for snow. The youngest of six siblings, she has four brothers and one sister, two of whom have devoted their lives to ministry. Cris now lives in Northeast Michigan with her husband, Les, and their loyal dog, Cookie. You can connect with Cris on Facebook under the username Cris Hoxie Author, and follow her at https://authorcrishoxie.wixsite.com/authorcrishoxie. She is also the author of *Embracing the Armor of God*.

Read more at https://authorcrishoxie.wixsite.com/authorcrishoxie.